Lauren had forgotten just how carefully they'd buried it. Or where. But she was determined to find it.

She ripped off the plastic casing. And now the treasure – their scroll – all neatly tied up with red ribbon. She'd forgotten the ribbon but not the words on the scroll:

'We, the undersigned, swear to stay together, defend each other and defeat our enemies.'

And underneath their signatures, each joined to the next to show how they could never be separated.

The scroll had been untouched for years. But now Lauren stabbed away at each letter until there were just tiny holes on the scroll where his name had been.

Pete Johnson has a panel of readers across the country whom he canvasses for opinions. Here's what some of them say about *No Limits*:

'This is compelling to the cliff-hanging end. It is effective in capturing the views and lifestyles of young people today. The story is strong, well-rounded and well-written. I was incredibly impressed.'

'The story is really warm and I liked the theme; it's the sort of friendship everyone dreams of but seldom finds. My favourite character is Cathy. I know her animal rights beliefs are something a lot of people feel strongly about . . . Jez is another fascinating character . . . I thought all the characters were realistic and special.'

'Jason is the one I most identify with. He's a brilliant character . . . someone I'd like to know.'

PETE JOHNSON

FRIENDS FOREVER

Teens · Mandarin

First published in Great Britain 1991
by Teens · Mandarin
an imprint of Reed Consumer Books Limited
Michelin House, 81 Fulham Road, London SW3 6RB
and Auckland, Melbourne, Singapore and Toronto

Reprinted 1992

Copyright © 1991 Pete Johnson

ISBN 0 7497 0607 4

A CIP catalogue record for this title
is available from the British Library

Phototypeset by Intype, London
Printed in Great Britain
by Cox & Wyman Ltd, Reading, Berkshire

Contents

With love and special thanks to Jan, Linda, Hilary Lapedis, Anthea Morton-Saner of Curtis Brown; Martin Heffron, Annabel Mayes, Ashley Noble, Lisa Farron, Simon Slater, Karen Hackett and those esteemed readers: Clare Slack, Emma Jones, Mick Ward, Marie Knight.

'Friendship, another shared dream, something the participants have to believe in and put their faith in, trusting that it *will* go on forever.'

Raymond Carver

Sabotage at Lauren's Party

Lauren didn't think anyone had seen her run away. She hoped not. Running away from your own birthday party was deeply shaming. But if she'd stayed any longer she'd only have started crying, and she had far too much style for that. She'd just rushed out, without even telling Cathy, her long-time best friend.

Lauren had spent so long planning this pool party, too, even managing to get her parents out of the house for the whole evening. And just before eight o'clock she had switched on all the lights round the pool, then threw in a few sprays of white carnations – Mum's idea. And all at once the pool wasn't its usual murky green any more but a blue, so rich and deep, that Lauren just knew tonight was going to be special . . .

Now it was pitch dark, not even a moon, and the

sky seemed about two feet above Lauren's head. But she still wasn't crying. She wasn't even sad any more. Instead – and this was most strange – she felt amazingly energetic. She remembered this boy in her class who had swallowed so many energy tablets he'd leapt on to his bike and cycled over thirty miles to London. Well, that's exactly how Lauren felt. Lauren, the girl who always skived off cross-country, suddenly could run forever. She'd raced through Dell wood and across the meadows where the horses were, just like she'd done hundreds of times before.

And here it was, just as she'd left it, an old workman's hut rotting away in the middle of nowhere. This was their hut and even though they hadn't been back for a year at least, their combination lock still protected it. 777, those were the magic numbers. Her idea. Jason had wanted 666, after all there were six of them he'd argued. But she'd said 666 was unlucky and everyone had agreed with her. For once Jason had been defeated. She smiled faintly at the memory.

As soon as she stepped inside time started twisting about, just like she'd hoped it would. For she was baling out of tonight and going back . . . back to when this had been their own secret meeting place. It reeked of dust and stale air and all the windows had boards over them, so it was always dark and shadowy and mysterious. And yet, it was

2

also the one place where you felt no one could ever find you. Here you were always safe.

And the darkness was oddly soothing. She yawned and stretched. There was the old gas stove which they'd tried to clean out and almost blown themselves up in the process. There was the lino, which Adam had bought, and that broom. They'd sprayed across the wall – THIS IS PRIVATE PROPERTY AND BELONGS TO JEZ, LAUREN, ADAM, MARK, CATHY, and JASON (BLAZE)–BLAZE! *He* had to give himself two names of course. How pathetic can you get.

'Blaze,' she repeated, her voice full of contempt while a tear escaped down her face. Now she could cry if she wanted to. But instead, she just slumped on to the lino. Tonight Jason had been so evil to her. That's the only word to describe it. And she didn't know why. There was no reason for it. But then people do that don't they. They sneak into your heart and then just when you're least expecting it, smash it up.

She stood up. She was shaking now. A crazy idea had erupted. She hesitated for only a second.

Cathy was late. Lauren had hissed, 'Cathy, see you upstairs in five minutes,' at least fifteen minutes ago. But Cathy had been delayed by this guy she'd caught stealing C.D.s. He hadn't been invited of course. And yet he'd come prepared with a huge rucksack for all his plunder.

So now Cathy was rushing up the stairs. Not that she usually moved so quickly for one of Lauren's summons. Lauren always seemed to be saying, 'Got to talk to you, Cath, urgently.' And then she and Lauren would spend all the lunch-hour whispering away in the loo about a guy Lauren would have totally forgotten a week later. Cathy was getting more than a bit sick of it, to tell the truth.

But this was different.

Tonight, Cathy had been as stunned as Lauren by what Jason had done. It didn't make any sense. And Cathy just couldn't figure out why Jason, Lauren's boyfriend for seven weeks (a record for both of them) should decide to walk into Lauren's fifteenth birthday party with a girl no one had ever seen before, draped over his arm.

As they approached the pool Cathy could feel Lauren gripping her arm tightly. And there was a hushed, thrilled silence as everyone gathered around for a big scene. But Lauren, in fact, was marvellously controlled, just cried, 'Hello Jason, I didn't know you had another sister,' which Cathy thought was pretty good, considering it was such a shock. Cathy had, in fact, been waiting for Jason to say that this was his long lost cousin or something. There must be a logical explanation for this. But there wasn't.

Then Jason and this girl strutted over to say

hello to Mark and Adam, both of whose faces were still frozen with amazement, while Lauren turned to Cathy and whispered, 'Did you see what she was wearing – only cycling shorts with a fluorescent line down the middle – oh please.' But then she suddenly said, 'Cath, what's he doing this for?' and she sounded so bewildered and so hurt that Cathy's eyes started smarting.

Cathy moved the chair, blocking the top of the stairs, her idea, just so everyone knew it was private up here, opened Lauren's bedroom door and then let out a low gasp.

A guy with about five hundred tattoos sprung up from the bed, followed by a small, blonde girl.

'You're not supposed to be here, you know,' said Cathy, looking somewhere over their heads. 'So do you mind going downstairs, I'm meeting someone here,' she added. Then she stood completely still, just like teachers do when they're ordering you out of a classroom at lunch-time. Neither of them moved at first but then they started moving in a kind of slow motion – just like people do who are being chucked out at lunch-time, the guy tut-tutting. As they passed Cathy, the girl half smiled and said, 'I hope he's nice.'

After peeking into the other rooms, Cathy returned to wait for Lauren and then, without really thinking, started straightening the covers on the first bed. There were two beds – twin beds – here. And when Cathy stayed over, which she did very rarely as she only lived about five minutes away, she'd use the other bed, the one now covered with jackets. She envied Lauren those twin beds and the built-in wardrobes and all this space (her room was barely big enough for one bed). But she'd never felt especially comfortable in here. Perhaps because it was just too carefully designed. She could imagine little groups of people trailing around it. 'And this is our pale pink showroom.' There were far too many mirrors, all ready to pounce on you and expose your less-than-perfect looks.

She moved a couple of jackets and sat down. The party was getting very noisy. Lauren was probably busy trying to keep everyone in the garden. For the plan was, that no one would actually go into the house. But there were just too many gate-crashers to control. She and Jez had said there should be people on the door but Lauren just kept repeating, 'It's not that sort of party.' Well, it was turning into that sort of party. Poor Lauren. What a mess of an evening. Should she try and find her? Cathy stood up. Then she heard a strange rumbling sound like thunder coming from downstairs. What was that? Cathy didn't feel quite brave enough to find out. Besides, it was probably better if she waited here where Lauren could find her.

She stood and stared at the pinboard. This was the one area where Lauren could put up her own pictures. And there they were, the usual colour snaps of Tom Cruise, Emilio Estevez and Matt Dillon doing their millionth cute smile of that day. Only wiping out most of Tom Cruise's smile and half of Emilio Estevez's were two large black and white photographs of Jason. They were the ones of him waving his latest swimming trophy in the air, which the local paper had featured a couple of weeks ago. Only these photos were blown up. Lauren must have ordered them specially.

Cathy stared at his broadly grinning face. He looked good in a photograph. But then it would be amazing if he didn't. Normally Cathy had a lot of time for him and they'd been friends – good friends – for so long. But you can know someone for years and they can still shock you. Just what was he playing at tonight?

It was then she heard a sudden roar of chanting from the garden, followed by monstrously loud clapping and cheering. What had happened now? Clearly something awful. Cathy ran out of the room and down the stairs.

Mark and Adam stared into the pool at the upturned sofa. The experience was one Adam could only compare to that of seeing your head-master rolling around in the gutter one Friday night yelling, 'Get em off,' to anyone who walked past. It was really quite shocking seeing that leather sofa in such an undignified position.

And to think, Adam had sat respectfully on the

7

edge of it only last week and distinctly uncomfortable it was too. Still, that sofa was more for gazing at admiringly and murmuring, 'About January 15th, 1836,' than sitting on.

And then Adam kept tuning into his parents saying, 'These people offer hospitality, so how can they treat their house like that.' All evening he'd been trying to shake his parents off. But it was no good. They weren't wanted but somehow they still kept popping into his head. Then he thought of Lauren's dad. Even when he was being friendly, he was pretty scary. So when he sees what's happened tonight . . . poor Lauren. But the two guys who had done the sofa throwing didn't seem the least bit concerned. Instead, they were clapping and laughing and being patted on the back as if they'd just won the star prize in some crappy game show.

Who were they? Adam was certain he'd never seen them before. Yet they were dressed identically to about a dozen other guys here, in tatty jeans, ray-bands, very short spikey hair. He didn't recognise any of those either. They were clearly humanoids, programmed to wreck parties. Mark began imagining armies of these humanoids sniffing out parties across the country – no party could escape them.

'We should have stopped them,' murmured Mark.

'How?'

Adam shook his head. Then they both sat down

8

again at one of the little tables by the pool. Even the plastic flowers had a defeated air about them. Adam looked around. Was a girl on the table opposite, staring at them? She seemed to be. Well, he'd let Mark have her, as he always did now.

The girl got up. She was walking towards them.

'Mark, see that girl on your nine o'clock, I think she's giving you the eye.'

'Where, where? I don't see her.' Mark was almost yelping with excitement.

'Yes you do, she's on your seven o'clock now and I really think you could be in there.'

Now Mark saw her. He leaned forward, catching her eye. He was good at this part. It was the rest of it he found tricky. Jason, the world's leading expert on this, had once explained to him, that you can tell if a girl's interested by the way she looks at you. It was all to do with a greater openness in the pupils. The trouble was, Mark didn't think he'd noticed that in any girl's pupils. So he was still rather vague about what to look for. Still, it was worth a try.

He stood up, making himself at least four inches taller. And right away he noticed the girl turn her attention away from him and on to a boy over his left shoulder. He quickly sat down again.

'A real Sharon, that one. Don't know how she got into Lauren's party. In fact, I don't know how half of them got in.'

9

There was a sudden squeal as yet another person got pushed, fully clothed, into the pool.

Adam shook his head. 'Should have had us on the door,' he said. Then he peered at Mark curiously. 'What have you been doing, shaving your eyebrows or something?'

'I had to, man,' said Mick. 'They were getting really bushy and joining right across my eyes. It looked as if I was turning into a werewolf,' he paused.

'Well, you've got this dirty red mark right above your nose now.' Then seeing Mark's startled face he went on, 'I suppose it's only really noticeable when people are up close to you, though. It's not really bad or anything. Not like that guy at our school who got one of his eyebrows burnt off. His eyebrows went all crinkly and just . . .' He stopped, Cathy had briefly joined the crowd round the pool and now she was making for them. She looked just like she did at the end of an exam, all anxious and sweaty.

To try and cheer her up, Mark called out 'Hey, Cathy, like the bare flesh.' He pointed at her tight red dress which finished just above the knee. Normally she flushed with pleased embarrassment at compliments. But this time she just said, 'Oh don't. I left it in the dryer too long. Does it look really awful?'

'No, it look great, doesn't it?' said Mark.

'Yeah, dead horny,' said Adam.

Cathy half-smiled, 'I wish.' She had few illusions about her looks. On a good day, which this wasn't, she looked all right but horny, never. 'I nearly came in my tatty old jeans only I knew Lauren would kill me.' Then she looked around at all the gate-crashers in their tatty jeans and half-smiled again.

'You saw what they did with the sofa?' said Adam.

Cathy shuddered. 'Her dad is just going to blow his circuits when he sees that. They're all over the house too. I caught this guy about to make off with all their C.D.s.'

Adam shuddered. That shudder belonged to his parents, of course. Even at a party he couldn't lose them. They were the reason this party wasn't on a Friday as Lauren had wanted. For he had to spend every Friday night with them seeing in the Sabbath. It was Mark who asked Lauren to change the day of her party. Adam was just too embarrassed even to mention it. And Lauren was really good about it. She went on about how the party wouldn't be the same without him and anyway, it was boring having parties on the same day as everyone else. She was just incredibly understanding actually, which made Adam feel awful.

Tomorrow night, when most normal people hold parties, he'll have slipped back into his other life. And he'll watch them light the candles and have his chicken soup and . . . act as if nothing has changed. What else can he do. For he'd tried arguing with them. Once he got really mad with them. He cried, 'If we can watch television on Friday night why can't I go out, what's the difference, come on, tell me?' He was practically yelling at them and they just sat and looked at him with such hurt and bewilderment.

That's why Adam doesn't tell them anything now. Or rather, he tells them little lies. When he's going to a party or the pub he'll just say he's round Mark's working on a history project. That's what he's supposed to be doing tonight. It's as if he has two quite separate identities and sometimes that can be quite exciting. Most of the time it was just a pain though. For it meant he had to leave parties insanely early, remove any incriminating evidence (like jelly from the jelly fight he'd had at another party last week) and answer all the questions beginning with, 'What did you have to eat?' Why did they always begin with that question? He looked around him again.

'Cathy, do you want us to do anything?' asked Adam.

'I just want to find Lauren,' said Cathy. 'I haven't spoken to her since Jason . . . I've been waiting for her upstairs but she seems to have disappeared. You haven't seen Jez, have you?'

Adam shook his head.

'I just thought she might be with him.'

Jez felt awful. So he made himself a cup of coffee,

which he managed to spill all over the creamy-white carpet in the hall. Still, if you have a white carpet at a party, well you're asking for it, aren't you. Someone will throw up all over it before the evening's ended anyway. Unavoidable. Law of the universe. Jez peered into the lounge. It was dark and murky and very smokey. The one thing Lauren wanted to avoid was smoking because she hated it, her parents hated it, and it turned the walls yellow. So Jez had restrained himself all evening. Only now the party was full of people he didn't know, smoking their heads off. And he hadn't got even one fag. So he'd have to die quietly in the corner instead.

But he'd hardly closed his eyes before he felt someone shaking him.

'Jez, are you awake?'

'Possibly.' He looked up. It was Adam.

'Jez, you haven't seen Lauren, have you?'

'No, sorry. By the way, you couldn't splash us a fag, could you mate?'

Adam shook his head. 'Jez, Cathy's getting really worried. She's afraid something's happened to Lauren.'

Jez struggled to his feet. Lauren wasn't the kind of person who went in for disappearing, and certainly not from her own party. In a way, this was all his fault. He shivered. No, Lauren will be all right. She'll come waltzing back any second now.

'Listen,' said Adam.

13

'What.'

'Exactly, the music's stopped.'

And then they saw Cathy and Mark signalling to come over. They were huddled conspiratorially together, a little way from the pool, where half the party was still gazing down in wonderment at that sofa. They'll be taking photos next, Jez thought, and then they'll start taking bits off the sofa for souvenirs, just like they do at plane crashes.

'Cathy, did you switch the music off?' asked Adam.

'Yes,' said Cathy. 'And I've rung the police.'

'So they'll be here about ten o'clock tomorrow,' muttered Jez.

'But we've got to stop the party now,' said Cathy. 'Lauren was having a mental breakdown about ash burns on the carpet so when she sees this . . .'

'But how exactly do you stop a party,' asked Adam.

Jez grinned. 'You say, ladies and gentlemen, I hereby declare this party closed. I do hope you enjoyed gate-crashing by the dozen and trashing Lauren's house . . .' He stopped. Cathy was giving him one of her looks.

'We could tell them that I've called the police,' said Cathy.

'Yes, that might make a few go. But who's going to tell them?' Jez asked.

'Me,' said Mark. 'I'll tell them.' Mark tried to twist his face into a scowl. But even he couldn't hide the dimpled looks and curly blonde hair which sent Cathy's mum into a swoon every time she saw him. And Adam's mum too – and every mum in Cartford, probably.

'He looks just like that little boy on the Sugar Puffs ad,' Cathy's mum said once. It was a long time before Mark forgave her for that.

'I'll say it,' repeated Mark, a little more quietly this time, his face fish-belly white. Cathy gave Jez another look.

'No, I'm the oldest and the drunkest,' said Jez. 'I'll do it.'

He looked around. 'No sign of Jason, I suppose.'

'No, he left ages ago with that girl,' said Cathy.

She was feeling extremely cross with Jason tonight yet she couldn't help wishing he was here now. There was no one like Jason for coping with emergencies.

'Okay then,' said Jez. 'I'll say it. Hold my can will you, Adam, for if it's any nearer the power of my voice will crack it open.' He gave another little laugh. Then Cathy gave him a kiss on the side of his face.

'What's that for?' asked Jez. 'Don't tell me, you can't keep your hands off me, I know.' He gave yet another little laugh as the four of them edged closer together. Then he whispered, 'Here goes nothing.' He clapped his hands. 'Ladies and gentlemen, we've called the police and they'll be here in five minutes. SO WILL YOU LEAVE NOW.' Then with a sudden flash of anger he added – 'GO AND WRECK YOUR OWN HOUSE. THIS PARTY IS OVER!'

Lauren had forgotten just how carefully they'd buried it. Or where. She'd been ages turning over all the rocks and stones by the hut. But she was determined to find it. At last, here it was. She ripped off the plastic casing. Then she tore open the envelope. And now, the treasure – their scroll – all neatly tied up with red ribbon. She'd forgotten the ribbon but not the words on the scroll: 'We the undersigned swear to stay together, defend each other and defeat our enemies.' And underneath, their signatures, in order of age and each joined to the next to show how they could never be separated and underneath, their names in capitals.

JEZ STEPHENS, ADAM ROSEN, CATHY ADAMS, MARK APPLETON, BLAZE (JASON) KENT, LAUREN DAVIES.

With the words, 'This is a legal document, binding

the aforementioned to remain 'FRIENDS FOR-EVER.'

She smiled now at the words 'legal document' and at the way they'd tried to disguise their childish writing by making it all loopy. She'd been in clubs before of course. And two weeks was the longest any of them had lasted. For once you'd made the badges, said the passwords and decided who could – and best of all who couldn't – be a member, it was just boring. Except this one. Even then she'd known this one was special. Perhaps because it wasn't a club at all really. It was more a pact, us against everyone who went to Palin Comprehensive, which was everyone in our village. Except us. We were the outsiders, the foreigners, the aliens. For we went to Farndale School, just two miles away in Cartford town centre.

Farndale School reckoned itself. Everyone who went there had to wear sick-making blazers and when the boys played cricket, they had to wear these girls' hats from 1940. Yet the school also had the best exam results in the country, which many of the parents (and none of the pupils) thought was due to a headmaster Mr Nuttley (or Nut-out), who looked as if he had died two weeks ago. He'd swirl into one of his regular emergency assemblies, treating anyone who dared cough in his presence to a stare Freddy Krueger would have envied. Then his voice would tremble with rage as he'd say, 'I can only think this is some kind of sinister

JOKE' before tucking into this week's horrific crime – WEARING TRAINERS.

Despite these brain-numbing interludes it was a pretty good school with a large waiting list.

At first she'd walked home with Cathy just for someone to walk home with. She'd thought they were too different to be friends. But then suddenly their friendship started growing. Lauren doesn't think it's ever stopped. Once when her mum had asked Lauren why she and Cathy were so close, she'd replied, 'Because Cathy is the most untwo-faced person I know.' That said it all, really.

Mark they both liked right away. In fact, as Cathy said, 'they'd adopted him.' Most nights he'd walk home with them and Lauren loved it when he'd try and show off, saying, 'No good-looking guy ever stole the limelight from me you know.' And they'd look down at him – for when he first started school he was so minute you could almost stamp on him – desperately fighting back their laughter. Poor Mark, he always tried so hard. Jason was his hero, of course. He was usually with them too.

But Adam they didn't know until a bit later. He was really shy. And Lauren remembered the embarrassed way he'd slink off to the library when they had assembly. Until one day she'd said to him, 'I really envy you missing Nut-out's assemblies,' and they'd got talking and that night he walked home with them. Then, of course, he and Mark became like a team – with Adam always a good head taller than Mark.

As for Jez, he was a year older than everyone else. But he'd joined the school the same time as they had after moving from Derby (and gaining a dazzling 90% in an exam). Somehow Jez seemed able to escape from school earlier than anyone else. Often they'd meet him in the cafe where he'd be stuffing himself with carbohydrate and tobacco. So then there were six of them. And right from the start the local kids hated these aliens in their bright red blazers. But no one realised quite how much until one afternoon . . .

Mark was late home from school – and alone – when he got caught by the posse, as the local kids liked to call themselves.

'Been to your violin lesson, have you?' they jeered.

And before Mark could answer, 'No, football training,' they were on to him. It was about forty to one and they left Mark in a heap of blood and pain. They'd broken his arm and wrist but worst of all, they'd taken photographs of his annihilation. For weeks Mark would suddenly say, 'Those pictures of me, I bet they're looking at them right now . . .' until finally Adam, Jez and Jason broke into Bonehead's home while she and Cathy acted as lookouts. Never had anything seemed quite so vital as getting those photographs back. They turned the house upside down. Never found them.

Perhaps Bonehead has them even now, wherever he is. His family left the area soon after. He got expelled from Palin for pushing someone through a window, didn't he? Lauren wasn't sure. But he was really crazy that boy. And all during the first year, when he was leader, they always walked home together. And if Lauren had to stay behind for detention or something, two of the boys would always wait for her. She smiled at the memory of the boys either side of her, her own personal bodyguards escorting her to the hut.

By the middle of the second year the aggro started to die away. But every day after school they still all left together, and they still always stopped off at the hut. Adam was first to bring things – a lino, cushions, hundreds of tapes, even pictures. 'We've got to make it our place,' he said. Jez kept a supply of drink there, called it Jez's bar. She remembered him teasing her about her favourite drink, a mixture of wine and lemonade. 'That's a funny drink,' he said, 'Half a woman's drink, half a little girl's.' It was still her favourite drink. Jez of course, drank more than everyone else put together. And Lauren could remember them all carrying him home at half-past five in the afternoon. Not that his parents seemed too bothered.

She stood up. When had they stopped coming here. Wasn't sure. It wasn't like an official ending. Although, by the end of the third year, Robin, her then boyfriend, was picking her up from school in his car. But she still went to the hut occasionally, still felt part of the group.

And then there was the terrible time in March this year when they heard that Lisa, Adam's girlfriend, had been killed in a car crash on the motorway. Lauren didn't know her very well but she remembered her at Adam's *bar mitzvah*, laughing at what Jez had written in Adam's card. She was just bursting with life and fun then. Who would think that two years later all that life could be extinguished, just like that – and in the afternoon too. Somehow, Lauren always imagined car accidents taking place late at night, not on lazy, sunny afternoons. And afterwards Lauren couldn't even bear to look at Adam at first. She just felt so sorry for him – and so guilty somehow.

Adam's parents were kind and sympathetic but they didn't understand how deeply the pain had gone inside him. They thought he was getting over it. But Mark knew he wasn't. And when one night he couldn't get an answer on Adam's phone, he tore round, forced open the door and found Adam upstairs in the bathroom. He'd passed out trying to slit his wrists. That night, Lauren couldn't stop shivering. Then Cathy came round, and later Jez, and they just sat huddled together waiting for Mark and Jason to get back from the hospital.

The next time she saw Adam – they'd set up this rota so he'd never be on his own – he was sitting in the hut listening to The Doors with a glazed look on his face. That look has never really left his face. She remembered something else. The envelope. Inside the envelope they'd each placed something for posterity. And Adam had put in – yes, here it was – the little silver ring which Lisa had given him. She'd also given him a beautiful gold ring, a kind of secret engagement ring he called it – he still wore that.

What else had they put in that envelope? She pulled out an empty crisp packet. Jez for sure. And then her offering, a make-up pencil and a photograph she'd taken of the five of them, arms all round each other. Cathy had her mouth open as if she were saying something, she was also wearing a truly appalling flowered dress. Adam was grinning broadly and looking so genuine – and wasn't his hair short then, it was almost down to his shoulders now. And next to him was Mark, with his 'Oh gee' grin and head tilted forward slightly as if he were waiting for a race to start.

Jez hadn't changed at all. But then he was a year older than everyone else. He was grinning away in his old woollen jumper and tatty mac. Funny, whatever Jez wore never seemed to have any colours in it. Everything blended in together to form a natural nothing.

And lastly and now leastly, there was Jason in those black trousers with zips all over the place, leather jacket hanging off his back, an 'I'm so wonderful' smirk on his face. 'Oh, Jason,' cried Lauren suddenly, 'you're a real Mr Confidence, aren't you. And you're so pleased with yourself. Well Jason – ' she shouted out into the night air – 'I'm about to wipe that smile off your face forever.'

'If I saw Jason now, I really think I'd kill him,' Cathy announced.

Jez stopped walking. 'Not kill him, surely.'

At this, an image of Jason grinning mischievously flashed through her head. Cathy faltered. 'Well no, not exactly kill, I'd settle for tying him to an electric chair and give him a few jolts. But I could definitely do that.

'But, Cath, you know Jason, he probably didn't think it was any big deal.'

'What, to walk into Lauren's party with his arms all round another girl is no big deal. Come on, Jez, even you can't defend Jason this time.' Cathy's voice shook a little, just like it did when she was talking about animals being used in experiments.

'Anyway, let's speed up a bit,' she went on, 'Mark's on his own at Lauren's and we promised we'd be back before her parents.'

'Mark'll be all right. I told him all he's got to do is protect her parents from anything which might seem dubious, like the inflatable lino in the back garden with shaving foam all over it.'

'And how does he do that?'

Jez considered this. 'Well, the best way, I reckon,

would be to meet them at the door and then blind-fold them.'

'You're a great help.' A smile escaped across Cathy's face, then she became more serious again. 'We were just so lucky those neighbours had called the police too. If they hadn't turned up when they did . . .' she shuddered, 'Lauren's not going to forget tonight in a hurry, is she?' 'Jez, do you think she is at the hut?'

'Must admit I'd never have thought of looking for her there. Somehow I can't see Lauren hiking through the woods in her black dress.'

'Actually she was wearing mustard flares. Boys never remember what we wear. For which, in my case, I'm quite grateful.'

'You look okay to me,' said Jez.

'Compliments, compliments.'

'All right, you look beautiful – hey, hang on, why are you walking so fast?' he puffed after her.

'Because you're annoying me,' said Cathy, 'I hate it when you're all sarky.'

'Actually I wasn't being sarky. I do think you . . .'

'Let's change the subject, shall we?'

There was silence until Jez said, 'You ever been back to our hut?'

'Yes, once or twice. That's why I thought Lauren might.' She shrugged her shoulders. 'Otherwise I haven't a clue where she is.' She clenched her fists, 'Oh, Jason, you've caused all this. And you should be sorting all this out now.'

Jez didn't say anything. He was sorry for Lauren too, of course he was. But he couldn't help remembering a time, earlier this year, when he and Lauren had been together, making what he thought were serious squelching noises. Yet, the following night she rang him to say she'd met some chinless wonder who'd invited her out to a ritzy nightclub and acted as if Jez should be really pleased for her. So had Lauren seen him just as a friend all along, even when they'd got off together.

He thought about this a lot and kept hoping that somehow he and she might – well, he just kept hoping – until he heard about Lauren and Jason – and he was really pleased for them, if none too pleased for himself. But he didn't say anything until last night. Jason was on his way home from Lauren's when they met – and Jez invited him back to sample some of his dad's homemade wine – which blew their heads off and they were sprawled across the floor talking and fooling about, until finally the conversation got round to Lauren.

They started by trying to work out just why she was more gorgeous than any other girl in Cartford. And Jez began describing her out loud, blonde hair, thin legs, quite big hips, soft arms, round face, huge green eyes with eye-lashes that were so long they made her look like a cartoon character and that whipped-cream voice ... it was somewhere around here that Jez felt his head suddenly growing hot. He was becoming feverish with longing. And then all at once he was telling about Lauren and him. It all tumbled out, only exaggerated, very exaggerated. Especially the last bit about how Lauren just dropped him. Jason didn't say anything and his expression didn't change but you could feel something happening to him. And by the time Jez realised he'd gone too far, Jason had gone.

Funny, earlier this evening Jez had meant to ring Jason. He really had. He had actually dialled the number. But then he lost courage. And now he felt distinctly sick. He wasn't into causing people grief.

Yet, he'd – just what had he done?

Lauren didn't so much rub Jason's name away as stick holes in it. She stabbed away at each letter with her make-up pencil until there were just tiny holes on the scroll where his name had been. And nothing happened while she did it. A shower of meteors hadn't melted her eyeballs. Voices out of nowhere hadn't murmured, 'Beware. Beware.' It was really silly of her to believe anything would happen. But she had broken the spell, and cast Jason out. Suddenly she imagined this scroll on Jason's doorstep, all wrapped up in a brown paper bag. And then she saw Jason unwrapping the scroll. He was in his leather jacket, just like in the photograph. Only this time he wasn't smiling. Instead, his face was all twisted with pain and disbelief. For things like this really mattered to him, especially as he'd been their leader.

Only now it was as if he'd never existed. And for Lauren, he really didn't exist anymore. He may have hurt her tonight. But she'd never give him another chance. He was wiped out of her life forever. She started burying the scroll again. Yes, one day he was sure to dig this up. Lauren only hoped she'd be around to see his face when he did.

When Jez shone his torch on Lauren she was huddled in the corner, her long blonde hair hiding the side of her face. And then she turned round. A face so full of sadness that it didn't seem like Lauren's face at all. But then it was like those television programmes where, with just a click of the fingers, someone snaps out of a trance and is themselves again.

'Cath, Jez, so-r-r-y,' Lauren could make one word last longer than a sentence. 'I just had to get away for a while and I didn't think anyone would miss me.'

And there it was, her familiar teasing smile. But when they'd first come in where had Lauren been? At first, no one mentioned tonight. They just let time curve backwards and laughed about all the days past while the wind rattled the windows and the smell of dust, damp and Lauren's perfume all mingled together. Then Lauren did talk about her party. And the girl Jason had brought.

'It was the way she looked at me, as if to say and who are you anyway.' Suddenly Lauren's voice was shaking with anger. 'And I thought, here she is, not even an invited guest cutting me dead at my own party. And did you see the cycling shorts she was wearing. I can't imagine anyone wearing those, especially someone whose legs are so hairy and . . .'

'Not while I'm eating,' murmured Jez. He'd found a bar of chocolate which had been maturing in his mac for about two years.

When Lauren had moved from slagging off Jason's girlfriend to Jason himself, Jez dropped out of the conversation completely. Cathy understood why. It seemed disloyal somehow. Especially here. For he was everywhere in this hut. Cathy could see him now at one of their meetings declaring if you weren't a friend then you were an enemy.

Once, years ago now, they were all in Cathy's back garden just messing about when this relic next door put his head over the fence and started ranting on about all the noise they were making. Actually he was making far more noise than they were – and they all thought he was out of order. But everyone was far too polite to argue, or so Cathy thought. The following day, though, Jason posted this relic a letter stating that he was an escaped mass murderer and would be coming to get him any day now. Well, the old guy got into a right state and took the letter around to Cathy's mum. When her mum discovered the source of the letter she went mad. 'You can't do that sort of thing,' she said and made them write an apology. Of course it was Cathy who wrote it, not Jason. He was all for causing the old guy more grief.

To his enemies Jason would do literally anything. There were no limits. Still he was a good person to have on your side. Life felt a lot safer – and simpler – with him around. And sometimes he could really surprise you. Cathy would never forget one morning, very early, when she discovered a dead baby bird just by the hut, and it really upset her to see the bird just left like that. Then Jason turned up and straightaway he started digging a hole for it. And then he picked the bird up so gently and whispered, 'We lay this bird to rest. Look after it God, forever.' Then Cathy placed a poppy on the top and the two of them just stood there until everyone else turned up. And when they heard about it they were sorry, too, but she didn't think any of them would have done what Jason did. Apart from Adam, maybe.

How could someone be so tender and so cruel. Just two days ago Cathy had watched Jason and Lauren leave for a special meal out. And they were both dressed up – Jason in a grey suit, looking so adult that Cathy imagined she was glimpsing them in about five years time, a young married couple. There had always been something simmering away between them. But it was as if they were waiting for the right moment. It happened suddenly at a rather boring party in the village hall and Lauren had announced that Jason had asked her out and she'd accepted. She'd announced it really casually but she was grinning from ear to ear.

'I've just been thinking,' said Jez suddenly, 'cause I'll try anything once. Out there's our special scroll. We buried it, remember. Well, I reckon we should have a look and see if it's still there.'

Lauren's breath caught in her throat. Jez'd called it our special scroll and she'd tampered with it. She'd no business doing that, had she? And they're going to be furious when they find out, aren't they? What had got into her? Her mum was always asking her that when she was little. And tonight, well something really had taken hold of her. Something so large and powerful she'd been compelled to do what it told her.

It was hard to believe she'd done it. She could still feel the anger but it was rock-hard now, like something that's been left in the freezer for a couple of months. And she didn't feel energetic any more, just very very tired.

'I bet it is still there,' said Cathy, 'because we put a curse on anyone who moved it. Remember.'

'No, I don't remember that,' said Lauren.

'Oh yes,' insisted Cathy. Actually it was Jason who did the cursing but she decided to omit that detail. 'We said whoever disturbs this sacred scroll will never have any happiness, instead they will . . .'

Lauren stood up. She had to stop them. 'Actu-

30

ally, I think I'd better go before my dad has half the police force out looking for me.'

She saw Jez and Cathy exchange looks.

'Just how wrecked is my house?'

'The sofa's the worst,' said Cathy.

'What's happened to that?' asks Lauren.

'Let's say it's had its first swimming lesson,' said Jez.

'What?' Lauren groaned. This was like one of those nightmares that just go on, getting worse and worse. Right now she couldn't imagine tonight ever ending.

'What else? No don't tell me. You will both come back with me.'

'No way. We're leaving you now,' said Jez. Then he grinned. 'Of course we're coming back with you – you silly old tart,' and he spoke so affectionately, Lauren suddenly flung her arms around his neck. Even though Jez looked like the kind of person you found skulking in dark corners, scrounging money, she was very fond of him. He was just so exactly like the brother she'd always wanted.

'You're going to miss me tomorrow, aren't you?' said Jez.

'Miss you, where are you going, petal?'

Jez winced. He hated it when she used words like petal to him and that silly accent she put on, so patronising. She obviously thought he was going to say Luton or somewhere, so he quite enjoyed her look of amazement when he announced, 'Berlin.'

31

'Berlin – but how?'

'A mate's got me a job there.'

'Doing what?'

He laughed. 'Dish-washing.'

'And you're going off just like that?'

'Thought I might as well.' He'd been thinking about it for a while. Then after Jason left last night, Jez knew he had to go off by himself.

'What did your parents say?' asked Lauren.

'They're not too happy about it,' said Jez. 'They want me to do 'A' Levels.'

'They're right. You're really good at English and German and . . . Oh Jez, you just can't throw all that away.'

'Yes I can,' said Jez quietly.

'He can always do them when he comes back,' said Cathy. She'd already argued about this with Jez. She didn't want him to go. Yet she sensed he was determined. For some reason he had to do this now. Perhaps he just needed to get away for a bit. She could understand that.

'Cathy, did you know about this?' Lauren was flapping about.

'Only today,' said Cathy.

'So I'm the last to know,' said Lauren dramatically.

'It was what you might call a sudden decision,' said Jez. 'And besides, I didn't want to ruin your party, and once you found out I knew you'd be weeping and wailing and tugging at my coat.'

'If anyone tugged at your coat it would fall to pieces,' cried Lauren. 'But you know I'll miss you.'

And as Cathy watched Lauren rolling her eyes at Jez and Jez clearly loving it, she felt ever so slightly out of it. She would miss Jez, too. She pictured him, hitchhiking to Berlin, with his battered backpack, bleary-eyed but smiling.

'You will come back though, won't you?' demanded Lauren.

Jez smiled. 'They'll throw me out soon enough.'

As they walked back Lauren thought, so we're starting to split up. I'm losing Jez. Was this my fault? By tampering with the scroll, have I broken the spell? No she was getting silly now. This day was jinxed long before she came here. Now it was almost midnight. She was pleased. All she wanted now was for this birthday to disappear. But first, she had to face her father.

Letters to Berlin – Strictly Confidential

Dear Jez,

I woke up to the sound of laughter. The postman laughing at your postcard. It's brilliant. Actually, we need a laugh around here, more about that in a moment.

But first, I'm really pleased you're in Berlin and working!! What's this about going on to Greece, though. You never mentioned this before. Please explain in your next letter (HINT, HINT).

To answer your questions about Lauren, we've had TRAUMAS here. You remember after her party (how could you forget) when her dad went tearing about the place, yelling, 'How could you do this to me?' Next day he wasn't talking to Lauren at all. Every time she spoke to him he said, 'Don't talk to me. I trusted you. Now I don't want to know you,' and turned his back on her. So did Lauren's mum.

Then, next morning, Lauren came down for break-fast to find this letter on the mat for her. As she picked it up her dad walked past snarling, 'Don't think it's money either.'

Would you believe he'd written her a letter. You'd have cracked up if you'd seen it, for it was typed up like a business letter, only it was all in capital letters, like he'd written it at the top of his voice. It began – 'THE FOLLOWING IS TO BE READ AND DIGESTED. I GIVE YOU EVERYTHING AND YOU THROW IT ALL BACK AT ME. THAT HURTS. I HAVE TO PUNISH YOU IN A WAY THAT IS GOING TO HURT YOU.' There's a page of this. Then on the second page are the punish-ments.

No. 1 All Lauren's money to be taken out of her account.

No. 2 Lauren's winter holiday is cancelled.

There are fourteen punishments – they go on to a third page.

Well, of course, Lauren was in a right state. At one point she even said 'I wish Jez was here. He'd cheer me up.' And then she was round my house late that night when she suddenly burrowed her head in my pillow and at first I thought she was laughing. But she wasn't. And do you know, I've never seen Lauren cry before. I noticed, too, and this sounds a silly thing, but Lauren hadn't painted her nails. Then she said, 'I think I'm cracking up, Cath.' And we just sat talking for hours. Sometimes she didn't make sense. Like she kept on about how she'd put a curse on herself. Then we spoke about Jason. 'With every other boyfriend,' she said, 'I keep thinking to myself is this it. Is this the best it gets but with Jason, I never thought that.' And I said, 'Well, let me ring him and find out why be brought that girl to your party.' I was pretty keen to know myself. But she became quite hysterical and said she knew why he'd done that. He was bored with her but now she was forgetting him.

That night I hardly slept I was so worried about her. Then next morning she was on the phone, laughing. She'd just found another letter from her dad. This one just said, 'ALL THE PUNISHMENTS HAVE BEEN SUSPENDED UNTIL THE NEXT TIME YOU ANGER ME.' The following night Lauren's parents took Lauren out for a meal. And Lauren's dad couldn't have been sweeter. 'I told him all about Jason and he was just so understanding,' said Lauren. I have a feeling her dad quite likes it when Lauren breaks up with her boyfriends.

So Lauren's back with her father!! but not Jason. She won't even talk about him now and said if I'm her friend I won't talk to him either. Well, I want to be loyal but I hate being blackmailed into doing things. Don't you?

Anyway, Jason rang me yesterday. He just said, 'Cathy, it's Jason. How are you doing?' I said, 'I'm fine. But what about Lauren?' He said, 'I rang her but she put the phone down on me.' This was news *to me and when I asked Lauren about it she snapped, 'Of course I put the phone down on him. He wasn't apologising or anything. In fact, he just spoke to me as if nothing had happened.'*

I can't blame Lauren for feeling like that but it does mean I've hardly spoken to Jason. And for all his posing about I do miss him. I've seen a bit more of Mark and Adam – we still walk home together sometimes. They both say 'Hello' and they're missing you. We all are.

So keep writing, won't you.

Take care,

Much love always.

Cathy XXXXXXX

P.S.   *I'm going for a waitressing job at Coopers Mill. Don't laugh. Remember when we got chucked out of there for wearing jeans.*

P.P.S.   the info about Lauren is strictly confidential.

December the something.

Dear Jez,

Thanks for your letter – and notice how quickly I'm replying. So you've been picking oranges in Greece, what a doss. And who is Yvonne who went with you? You must tell me everything, you know. You ask what's happening here. Well, I'll save the shock news about me UNTIL LATER.

Firstly, last night I went out for a secret dinner with Jason, Adam, Mark and this girl who I thought was Mark's girlfriend but can't have been because she left with someone else. Actually, I think Mark thought she was his girlfriend too. He got talking to her in a bus shelter and when she said her legs felt cold and would he mind rubbing them, he thought, this is my kind of girl. But Jez, she was awful. She kept saying when she went out with a boy she didn't expect to have to pay for anything and didn't I agree. I said, certainly not. If the boy's not earning any more than you, why should he pay for it all. Mark always picks the wrong girls. I'd like to fix him up with someone really nice. And Adam. Oh yes, bit of gossip. Jason is supposed to be going out with a twenty-three-year-old model but when I asked him he just laughed.

Of course, all evening I was terrified Lauren was going to walk in and scream at me for being disloyal. She and Jason still aren't talking. And it's so silly for it means you can't ever see them both together, and we're forced into two camps. In Jason's camp there's Mark (who still hero-worships Jason like crazy) and to an extent, Adam, while I'm in Lauren's camp. You are LUCKY being out of all this.

Meanwhile, I've just finished the most awful form of torture known to mankind called The Mocks. We're all crammed together in a room full of heaving breathing and coughing, not to mention teachers with squeaky shoes. And Nut-out keeps fluttering by in his black cloak.

Still, in assembly recently, I really thought he was

39

going to cry. For he announced, with a sob in his voice, that schools could no longer offer the range of 'A' Levels owing to falling roles in other schools, though not our school, of course. Someone cheered — and hasn't been seen since. I was planning to go to college anyway. And so was Lauren, who thinks everyone at Farndale School is just too juvenile for words.

Now, I shall keep you in suspense no longer — my shock news is — you know the waitressing job at Coopers Mill I wanted. Well, I got it. That isn't the shock news. Just be patient, Jez.

Last Wednesday I was at Coopers Mill and there were two guys there — one of whom had quite nice eyes I thought — and that's all I thought. I was just clearing up the table next to theirs when the guy with the nice eyes called across, 'Are you available on Friday?' I said, 'What does available mean?' after which he went red and looked away and I thought, Cathy blows it yet again. Next time I saw his table he'd gone and I was disappointed but I said to myself, that's life (or my life, self-pity bit). But then Marguerita, (another waitress there, great laugh) came steaming over, yelling, 'He's left you a message on his serviette.'

Just about everyone in the restaurant was watching me read his message, a little poem actually. And at the end he'd put his phone number and added in big letters, PLEASE PHONE TONIGHT IF YOU'RE INTERESTED. Well, I was interested but you know

*me, I messed about. Should I ring him or shouldn't
I. And all the girls in the restaurant were giving me
advice (no one was getting served). Then finally he
rang saying, 'I can't talk for long I'm on my portable
phone but I just wondered if you'd let me take you
out for a meal in town (meaning London).*

*Well, I said yes and it was wonderful and he is
so charming (even Lauren's a little jealous) and Jez,
prepare to thrown up, I'm in LOVE. I know it's a
bit quick and more than a bit corny but I just feel so
happy – AND THAT'S MY SHOCK NEWS.*

*Jez, must close. Are you coming home for Christ-
mas? YOU'D BETTER! But if you don't, have a
brilliant time. I know you will.*

Take care,
Love always,
Cathy. XXXXXXX

P.S.   Don't forget to send me a Christmas card.
P.P.S.   Have I told you how happy I feel?

Four Days to the Exams
My Dear Jez,

*It was great to hear from you AT LAST. Glad
you're back in Berlin and congratulations on your
promotion – waiter now. Next time you write I shall
expect you to be chief waiter – if not manager.*

*My news isn't so good. I was made redundant last
week. Coopers Mill was very sorry and all that but*

41

they are cutting back, so goodbye Cathy. They did give me a really good reference though.

As for Martin. I'm afraid he made me redundant some time ago. No reference either, just a phone call one night saying he'd met someone else – the usual – I'm afraid I made rather a fool of myself over him. I even said to him, 'If ever you want to come back or you've got any problems I'll be there . . . can you believe that. I just didn't want to let him go.

For weeks afterwards I'd race to the phone. Lauren was great. She said. 'If he does ring don't you dare speak to him. Make him sweat.' Anyway, he never rang or sweated and I'm over him. I'm not seeing anyone now and that's fine. What gets me mad though are all these cards that make love seem like a nice warm bath, all soft colours and pretty flowers. One day I'm going to design a card to show people what love really is. On the outside I'd have this hand stretching out to touch these live electric cables. Then, on the inside – it would be one of those pop-up cards – the hand all blown to bits, would spring out at you. What do you think?

Do I sound bitter or what?

You ask what Lauren's been up to. Well, having lots of flings. The night Mum and Katie were away Lauren stayed over at my house. And her new boy-friend, James Martin, was there. Do you remember him? He was in the year above you at school, very smart, works in a bank now (I know, Ugh!) Anyway, about eleven o'clock she sends James off saying, 'We're really tired now but be sure and give us three rings on the phone just so we know you got home safely. Well, he went off thinking what a nice, caring girl she is.

Meanwhile, Lauren is diving upstairs, giggling away, to get ready to go out to a night club with a guy called Ben. So when poor James gives his three rings, Lauren is already half-way to London!

Actually, I don't think she likes Ben or James very much. But you know Lauren, she has to have her fans. No, she and Jason still aren't talking. Only now they're making such a big show of ignoring each other.

It all seems so hopeless. And I wonder if the six of us will ever be together again.

Still, I've had some good chats with Adam. You can really talk to Adam, can't you. Even if a lot of the time he still seems far away.

'Half the time I'm not even on this planet,' he told me recently.

'So where are you then?' I asked. 'Somewhere good?'

'No, that's the problem,' he said.

Adam borrowed this friend's motorbike last week, went bombing off on it and got stopped by the police. They're not going to do anything but they went round his house and his parents were none too happy. You know they're quite strict anyway. Adam was actually laughing about it. Happiest I've seen him for ages. He said when he was roaring around on that bike he felt as if he could do anything, be anyone – there were no limits. Anything was possible. That's how we should feel all the time, isn't it? So why don't we?

And why do I still get so nervous and afraid of the silliest things. Sometimes, just going into a shop and asking an assistant for something takes all my courage. WHY IS THAT? Don't worry if you don't know the answer! I don't expect anyone does.

I've got a bit of very trivial news now – my mum is in lurve. And yes, I'd definitely like to send her one of my cards. She's going with this guy, Giles, who's really smooth and thinks he's the original cool dude. And he's just so fake. Lauren said he was probably just a fling and she should know! But then to give me a break from revising, Mum took my sister and me to Brighton, just for the day. And Mum said she felt really bad she couldn't take us away for a proper holiday but money really was tight at the moment with just her widow's pension and her little bit of money. Then she started saying how Giles might help us out. I was immediately suspicious. And Mum shut up after that, wouldn't say another word about it. But something's going on.

And as if I haven't enough to worry about with all my revising. Before I leave you and return to the social and economic effects of the Industrial Revolution (yawn, yawn) – one last piece of news – I am now a fully-fledged, lettuce-carrying VEGETARIAN.

I've always been a kind of vegetarian. Like, I've never been able to eat pork because I used to visit this farm where I'd play with all the little baby pigs. And they're just so cute. But then I got to thinking, if I'm not eating pigs why am I eating cows. Then a few weeks ago I passed the butcher's and saw all these pigs hanging up without their heads. It was the most disgusting thing I'd ever seen. And it seemed so unfair. What right have we to take away the lives of animals who are happy and healthy. No right.

Do you know, Jez, that butcher even had rabbits hanging up with their fur showing, so they'd just been freshly killed. If you passed shops with freshly killed humans hanging up, people'd soon start complaining. So why are animals different. Aren't they entitled to some dignity too.

That got me so mad I stormed over to the butcher and had a real go at him. Everyone in the shop could hear me. And he was shouting at me and in the end he tried to push me out of his shop. We picket his shop quite regularly now. We, being the animal rights group.

And Jez, I haven't eaten a piece of meat for five weeks. And honestly I think I'd die before I could eat meat again now. It would be just like eating human flesh. I'm going to try and make all my friends vegetarians too. So watch out!

But guess who's already in the animal rights group – JASON. I haven't seen him there yet – there aren't proper meetings again until August – but all the girls know him and think he's wonderful! When I told Lauren about this she snapped, 'Oh, he just steps into whatever's going. He'll be an anarchist next week.'

JEZ, WHEN ARE YOU COMING HOME? You realise it's almost a year since you left now, will be a year in August. (I don't think Lauren will be having a party this year!) Before we forget entirely what you look like, Please *come home.*

Now, Jez, I really must go and revise. Oh why is so much of my life so tedious?

Take care. Everyone says they'll be writing to you soon. But just remember who writes the most regular and the longest letters too.

With love, as always,

Cathy
XXXXXXXXXXXX

ONE YEAR LATER

Return of the
Human Dolphin

It is just eight-fifteen in the morning but already a chocolate sponge cake and a bottle of champagne are on the dining-room table. While around the table sits Lauren opening her birthday cards. Her parents are watching her. There is only one card left, the one her dad always puts at the bottom of the pile. She looks around anxiously. No sign of a present yet. The card says, 'Happy Birthday to a Wonderful Daughter' and inside – well Lauren never actually reads the inside – she is too busy picking up all the twenty-pound notes which fall out of the envelope.

'Count them. Count them,' cries her dad, leaping in front of her waving a camera. 'And look at me while you're doing it.'

Lauren beams at him, then continues. 'Four hundred and sixty, I feel as if I'm on a game show or something, four-hundred and eighty, five hundred, five hundred pounds.'

She hugs her father and mother and then her mother cuts the cake while Lauren and her father sit grinning at each other. He's a large man, whose bank balance, like his waistline, seems to be forever expanding. Despite his iron grey hair and smart suit, he looks more like a retired boxer than some-one who's very big in sales. Perhaps because he is sporting a most impressive squashed nose.

'This is really good of you,' says Lauren.

'Just so long as you're happy and appreciative of what we give you,' replies her Dad. 'That's all we ask. There is one very small condition that goes with the five hundred, though.'

Lauren's smile fades just a little and she puts her glass of champagne down.

'Your mother and I don't like you staying out late. Most weekends now we're sitting here waiting for you, sick with worry. And you know the time you're supposed to be home by, don't you?'

'Eleven o'clock,' mutters Lauren, turning away from him.

'That seems to us a perfectly reasonable time. That's why in future, Lauren, every time you arrive home later than eleven o'clock I will fine you fifty pounds.'

'Fifty pounds,' echoes Lauren disbelievingly.

'Yo baby, come on, light my fire,' murmurs Mark.

He is psyching himself up in a queue at Radleys, the gleaming new supermarket at the end of Cartford's gleaming new shopping precinct.

He looks across at his coach. But Adam is leaning against the door just staring into space, miles away. Adam's hair is way down past his shoulders now and he's wearing a prehistoric cotton shirt and deeply unfashionable jeans. Anyone can see he's just generally letting himself go. What Adam needs is a girlfriend. He could get one easily. Several girls have asked Mark about him. One said she thought Adam's long hair made him look really interesting, like a trendy poet or something. Perhaps Mark should grow his hair.

The queue moves one nearer the checkout. Maybe the girl behind the checkout will have a friend for Adam, too. First though, he has to get himself sorted out. He's going to just casually spin down the chocolates they've just bought for Lauren's birthday and then in a very light, cheeky Jasonesque way, remind the girl where they'd met before. And he'd add, 'Actually I'm going to Charades with some friends tonight. Would you care to join – what should he say, 'us or me'. 'Me' – it sounds more intimate.

When the woman in front finishes paying for all her dog food it'll be his turn. He's almost on. He looks across at Adam again. This time Adam sees him and gives him the thumbs up. Adam had tried to talk Mark out of this. He had a feeling the girl wouldn't remember Mark. And anyway, he didn't think this place, with its retina-cracking brightness and mind-rottingly jolly voices, reminding customers of this week's bargains, was the right setting in which to ask a girl out. So it isn't so much the outcome which surprises Adam, as its speed.

Before Mark has even had time to put his chocolates down, the girl is speeding off to the room marked 'Staff Only'. Mark stands gaping after her while Adam steams over.

Mark waves his hands like a defeated goalie, unsure just how the ball got past him. 'I'd only said, "Hello, remember me", before she goes, "Sorry, I'm on my tea-break now so I'm closing the till", and she was gone before I could say anything else. Yet she was really friendly before, wasn't she?'

Adam wouldn't describe a slight exercising of the lips across a crowded bar as really friendly but he just says, 'It's because she's in her uniform, Mark. And I know they're really strict about them talking to customers.'

'Yeah, yeah,' mutters Mark. 'She had her hair up too, doesn't look half so good like that.'

Then he flings the chocolates back. 'You can get 'em much cheaper in Bunces anyway.'

He smiles. He smiles again when an attractive if rather matronly woman opens the door and gasps. She's clearly not used to receiving human slime on the doorstep. He puts on his talking to the headmaster and elderly aunts voice.

'Oh, good morning. Is Lauren in, please?'

Recovering herself now, she says, 'Would you mind waiting in the hall while I go and see if she's available.'

Seconds later Lauren tumbles into view. When her mother had announced there was a tramp to see her, she should have guessed who she meant.

'Jez,' she cries. 'This is brilliant. But Cathy said you wouldn't be back for another month yet.'

He smiles. 'For once I'm early.'

'And you've gone all bearded. I like it. You look like a character out of an old Russian novel.'

Lauren hasn't changed, Jez thinks, same silvery laugh, same way of looking right into your eyes when she talks to you. She still knows how to set your heart thumping all right.

'Mum, you must remember Jez . . . he's been working in Berlin.'

'Oh really, how interesting.' Her Mum comes forward smiling bravely. Just treat these people as human, that's the secret.

'And what was your job there, Jez?'

'Dishwasher.'

'Ah,' another brave smile. 'Take your guest into the morning-room Lauren. And perhaps you'd like a drink, Jez.'

'I could murder a . . .' then he looked at Lauren's mum, 'a cup of tea.'

'And have you eaten?' she asks.

'Only a walnut, since breakfast,' says Jez.

As they journey to the morning-room Jez says, 'I bet you need a map to get around here, don't you. It is all right me coming here isn't it?'

'Of course, don't be silly.'

'It's just this feels a bit like Lady and the Tramp.'

'Oh Jez, you are funny.' She looks straight into his eyes. 'And I've missed you so much.'

All sorts of pleasurable sensations hurtle through Jez's body. If only she meant that.

Jez vaguely remembers the morning-room. He certainly remembers the marble fireplace, which he rather liked. But this time all the ornaments are out, so two huge brass lions now sit in front of the fireplace, while above it there's a shelf full of brass ornaments.

'I have to polish all the brass every Sunday,' says Lauren. 'Well actually I just polish the front bits. Anyway, sit down, make yourself at home.'

But as Jez chats away about his year in Berlin, Lauren stops listening. She's too horror-struck by what he's doing on the couch. He's picking the cushions up and pushing them on to the floor. And Mum and Dad get really up-tight about cushions being left on the floor. It's one of their things. Another is making sure all the bedroom doors are closed upstairs.

'That's better,' says Jez, sprawling himself across

the couch. 'So like I said, they finally figured I knew enough to be a waiter.'

Why couldn't he have told mum that instead of saying he was a dishwasher. And what was that about eating a walnut. Sometimes Jez isn't as funny as he thinks he is. And surely he could have at least taken the sleep from his eyes this morning – and when is he going to retire that scruffy old raincoat. Still it might have been worse, her Dad could have been here. He wouldn't have said anything to Jez's face but afterwards he'd have rushed about the room with the air freshener or something.

Jez chats on but he can tell Lauren isn't really listening. She's too busy staring at those bloody cushions. Well, cushions are for putting your feet on, everyone knows that. Jez could imagine his parents looking around this room and sighing over 'all the beautiful things'. They couldn't even afford those snooty-looking marble lions – which are just begging to be smashed up.

And his parents would be so humble, so pathetically grateful if Lauren's Mum gave them a cup of tea. 'She's so gracious,' they'd say, perched uneasily on the edge of their chairs. His dad had been a plasterer and quite a successful one, until, soon after they'd moved here, he fell off his scaffolding and strained his shoulder. He's worked at the land registry ever since. 'I'm just a penpusher now,' he says, with an apologetic laugh.

And late last night, when Jez saw his parents

again, he couldn't help noticing how small his dad looked. He was shrinking away before his eyes. One day soon he'll fit right inside his briefcase. The only time his dad seemed to expand a bit was when he showed Jez the new shelves he'd put up in Jez's bedroom and the new shower curtain in the bathroom.

Suddenly Lauren's mother bursts in with a bouquet of pink carnations.

'Just arrived,' she says.

Lauren snatches the card. 'They're from . . . oh Antony. Nice. Very nice of him.'

'Didn't think he'd forget your birthday,' says Lauren's Mum. 'Your tea won't be long,' she adds, giving Lauren a 'look' before disappearing.

'It's your birthday,' cries Jez.

'Ye-es'

'So it's exactly one year since . . .' their eyes lock for the first time. A jumble of images from that night flash though Jez's mind. Then in a kind of slow motion, he sees Lauren in that hut suddenly turning round and her face so full of hurt. Over and over he sees that moment until they're in each other's arms and Lauren doesn't care if her mother does catch her. She's seen the cushions on the floor and nothing can equal the horror of that.

Lauren starts feeling Jez's beard and making little moaning noises.

'Oh baby, I have missed you so much,' she whispers.

You're such a tease, thinks Jez admiringly.

'When I'm not skint I'll buy you something,' he says. 'Not that it will be easy. I mean, what can you buy the girl who has everything.'

'I haven't got everything.' Her tone is suddenly little girlish. 'And I get lonely and depressed sometimes.'

'What about your pink carnation fan?'

'Who, oh Antony, he's just someone I met in Portugal and he has been writing to me every day since. I wouldn't mind but he's a bit thick and doesn't understand about capital letters and full stops. He also thinks every 'b' needs a capital letter . . .'

'Why don't you help him then?' asks Jez.

'One day I will. I'll return one of his letters back with red pen all over it. That's what I'd love to do.'

'You're a hard woman.'

'No, I'm not. I'm a lovely woman. And stop laughing, Jez. I've a good mind not to invite you out tonight now.'

'Can't come anyway, got a date with this girl who keeps sending me pink carnations and who can't punctuate properly.'

'No you haven't, you're coming out with Cathy and me to celebrate my birthday and drown our sorrows about the G.C.S.E. results tomorrow. Oh yes – what's this Cathy said about you getting an "A" in English and German and French?"

'Just shows what rubbish exams are,' says Jez. 'I mean, if I can get an "A" anyone can.'

'I bet I don't. You are going to do "A" Levels?'

'No way,' says Jez quietly.

'Why?'

'Wrong time of the month.'

Lauren half smiles. 'Oh Jez, you can't go on just drifting around. What do you want out of life?"

'I'll tell you what I want,' says Jez. 'Have you ever seen dolphins swimming?'

Lauren nods.

'And they just glide, don't they, so easy, so effortless. No hassles. They also have brilliant sex lives.'

'So you want to be a dolphin?' Lauren's laughing again.

'Yeah, a kind of human dolphin. No stress, no aggro, just having a good time every day. No, the secret is to find a job that requires as little effort as possible. And I'll find one, maybe today. Then you can save all your energy for the important things in life, like, going out with Lauren. Where are we going by the way?'

'Charades.'

'That cess pit.'

'No, they've done it up. Supposed to be really good now. You will come, won't you? Mark and Adam are coming too. And Cathy.'

'How is Cathy?'

'Trying to get me to be a vegetarian.'

'She wrote me about that. And what about this guy, Martin?'

'All over a long time ago. She really fell for him. I was amazed actually. I mean, Cathy's always so sensible but then she – well like I say – she really fell for him.'

Jez nearly says, 'A bit like you over Jason.' But he doesn't.

He just asks, 'And Jason, will he be there?'

'Jason. Why should he be?'

Sometimes if you leave things they sort themselves out. That's Jez's theory anyway. But Jason and Lauren, they're just as they were, when he left. If Jez let himself he could feel mighty guilty about that. So good-hearted, amazingly genuine Jez has messed up Cartford's greatest love story. Maybe he should have stayed in Berlin a bit longer.

'You two still not talking then?''

Her voice becomes flat and toneless. 'As far as I'm concerned, Jason doesn't exist anymore.'

'Can we please get into a circle now,' asks the man with the rabbity teeth and shoes made out of carpet.

The dignified respectable members noiselessly move their chairs next to him, the schoolgirls follow, making rather more noise. Cathy finds herself at the end of this group and alongside the little old lady who thought this was a meeting about the poll tax, not animal rights.

Right at the back though, a small group remain

determinedly out of the circle. These are the hunt saboteurs or sabs as they call themselves. They huddle under their coats, whispering, smoking and blowing raspberries at the speakers. Their leader, Captain Andy, has long red hair and apart from the baseball boots, looks just like an ageing hippy. But it is Jason, their newest member who is lying across the table, his Doc Marten boots caked with mud, laughing loudly.

Jason's blond hair is shaved at the sides but much longer at the back now. He's given himself a small ponytail which Cathy doesn't normally like on boys. But it gives Jason a gipsy-boy look which really suits him – but then, what wouldn't. He's quite lean, but with muscular arms and a longish jaw.

Like Lauren, he has a face that you only expect to see on magazine covers and record albums. Perhaps that's why people just stop and stare at Jason in the street. Cathy's seen them do it, as if they can't believe their eyes. Even the girls here are turning round and giggling.

It's gone to Jason's head, of course. Hard for it not to, really. He'll strut about like Mr Macho at parties, acting like the kind of boy Cathy hates. But that isn't him, not really. At least she doesn't think it is. But then Jason is so hard to suss out. If there was one person's head she'd love to go inside it would be Jason's. She was sure there'd be some real surprises in there. For he keeps so much of himself hidden away. She remembered visiting Jason when he was getting over measles, a couple of years ago now. And his bedroom was really strange because it had nothing in it. Well there was a messy dressing table and a Walkman and cassettes but no pictures or little funny objects (Lauren's room is full of little furry koalas) or anything that might give any clues as to what he was really like. He has since painted all his bedroom walls black which says something, she supposes, but she's not sure what. And yet he can be such a good laugh. He certainly has the most bewitching smile. And then there was that time at the beginning of the summer holidays when he came to her first animal rights meeting, and they showed the most terrifying film she had ever seen. It was just one horrifying scene after another and Cathy thought she would have to leave – and when she saw this huge needle being poked into a cat's eye, she knew she would. So she got up to go and passed out instead.

And afterwards she felt so pathetic and so ashamed until Jason came up to her – they had hardly spoken since Lauren's party – and put his arms around her and said how he'd closed his eyes during most of that film too. He even insisted on walking her home afterwards.

She looks round. Jason is turning a copy of the newly-written constitution into a paper aeroplane. And then he looks up and his eye catches hers. He winks at her. And she wishes she were sitting at the back with him. That's where she should be. He was – no is – a friend. A special friend. And if it weren't for Lauren . . . She winks back at him. Surely even Lauren can't mind her doing that.

The old lady stands up and declares, 'All scientists are murderers.' The sabs applaud her wildly and the man with the rabbity teeth says, 'I'm sure we all feel like calling out things like that sometimes; anyway, to return to the constitution.'

Cathy can feel her ears folding over. He is very boring. And outside there are kids on skateboards and blaring music. Perhaps moving the meetings to the college wasn't such a good idea after all. Funny to think the next time she's in this hall will be on the first day of term for what's called 'Welcome and Registration', that's provided she gets the right grades of course. This had been the dark cloud that loomed over the whole holiday – and was now about to engulf her.

She knew she wouldn't sleep tonight. And she knew the post would be late tomorrow. Still, that was better than the alternative – the post being early and *him* sitting at the breakfast table, watching, gloating and giving his insincere smile. He doesn't care about me. In fact, Giles wants me and my sister out of the house, now he's moved in. He moved in yesterday afternoon. She deliberately stayed away. And when she came home in the evening he was stretched out in the lounge, television controls by his side as usual but nothing

62

actually seemed different – until much later – that night.

That was when she passed mum's room on the way to the bathroom. And mum always kept her door open a couple of inches, just in case Cathy or Katie needed her in the night. It was silly of her, of course, but reassuring too. Only last night, for the first time, the door was tightly closed. Between Cathy and her Mum now loomed a great barrier. And in the morning when the door finally opened, the stench of cheap 'splash it all over' after-shave polluted Cathy's room. She sniffs. Even now she can smell it on her clothes.

Suddenly something flutters just inches away from Cathy's feet. A paper aeroplane. She bends down, picks it up and sees on the outside in block capitals, WARNING – EXCITING MESSAGE INSIDE. Inside, there is a drawing of a pint glass with the words, 'FANCY A DRINK OR TWO AFTERWARDS, JASON.'

She peers at her embarrassingly old watch, nearly six o'clock already. So there'll only be time for a quick drink with him before she meets Lauren to go to . . .

Should she bother at all. It might be easier not to. Lauren would go mad for a start, and with good reason.

She reads the note again. If she says no, he might not ask her a second time. And Lauren has already cut him out of so many things this year. A rush of sympathy for Jason surges through her. And then she must admit, Lauren had rather annoyed her today when she rang Cathy at lunchtime to say Jez was back and round her house and would have put him on the phone only he was still eating. And Cathy thought, why is he round Lauren's house when I was the one who wrote to Jez every month with all the news. Lauren never so much as wrote him a postcard. Yet, as soon as he returns, it's Lauren's he rushes around to and he doesn't even come to the phone at first.

'I'll pull Jez to the phone later,' says Lauren smugly.

Everything just falls into her lap, Cathy reflects. That's why she suddenly turns round, points at the paper aeroplane and nods. And he looks so pleased. Cathy's heart misses a beat. She has no time for that soppy nonsense any more. But she does rather enjoy the way all the girls keep staring at her, so envious, so disbelieving. Of course, Jason could never think of her in that way. Just occasionally princes may marry commoners but good-looking guys can only go out with equally attractive girls.

In the same way, Cathy's partner will only be the male reflection of herself. Perhaps that's why she's never been very keen to meet him. And why, in fact, she'd rather just be a good friend to someone like Jason.

'All those in favour raise your hands now,' cries the man with rabbity teeth. Everyone seems to be raising their hands, so Cathy joins in, even though she hasn't a clue what she's voting for.

'So the minutes will read, that members agree the time is well overdue for another Radleys picket. Any proposals . . . ?'

Cathy turns round again. She's just had an idea for tonight. A brilliant idea.

2

Jason's Shock Appearance

Lauren is leaning over the balcony at Charade's and she is bored. Cathy knows this because she is also playing 'Pull a Pig'. This game begins by seeing who can make the longest eye contact with the grimmest bloke. 'Seven seconds,' squeals Lauren, 'seven seconds with the podge-master down there. I win.'

The podge-master thumps over to Lauren and Cathy. He is wearing a track suit and the kind of pink moon boots you'd only dare wear when there's two feet of snow outside. He is ruddy and fake-chummy and when he looks at Lauren, little globules of white saliva glisten at the corners of his mouth.

He insists on buying them drinks, 'Can't have beautiful girls like you getting thirsty,' he says.

He returns with drinks and a merry leer. 'There

you are Lauren,' he says. He turns to Cathy, 'And not forgetting Barbara, of course.'

'Barbara,' echoes Cathy. Does he really think she's a Barbara?

'Oh no, of course you're not Barbara, you're . . .' He hasn't a clue who I am, Cathy thinks. But then, he's hardly wasted a glance on me. Whenever she's out with Lauren, Cathy always feels like a badly taken photograph, permanently out of focus, more ectoplasm than human being. 'Actually, my name's Emily,' she says.

'Oh yes, Emily of course,' he splutters.

Lauren stifles a giggle.

'Cheers then, Lauren – and Emily.'

Cathy wouldn't have minded being mistaken for an Emily. For that conjures up a pale, fragile creature with blonde hair and green eyes, just like Lauren's. But Barbara – BARBARA!

'So what do you girls do, apart from have a good time?' he asks.

'We're air hostesses,' says Lauren.

His lips twitch excitedly. 'I've heard about you air hostesses.

'Oh, really,' says Lauren leaning forward, giving him the full treatment. 'What have you heard?'

He quivers the way fish do on the end of a line. But Cathy can't feel sorry for him. He's the kind of man who thinks buying a girl a drink entitles him to . . . She shudders at the very thought.

A jelly baby has more sex appeal than him and

most of the clammy people in that dark, smoky hole they call a dance floor down below. Last time she came to Charades everyone wore badges with smiling faces. Now most of the blokes are in skin-tight jeans which end halfway down their leg and the girls are in equally tight mini-skirts and white stilettos. Is there anything more hideous. Yes there is, she's just sighted a man in grey slip-ons. Grey, the colour that only ever looks right on those heavy, lumpy clouds that hover permanently above Cartford – and blend in perfectly.

She looks across at Lauren. 'Get rid of him,' she mouths. Lauren smothers a laugh. She won't be laughing soon, certainly not when she tells Lauren her brilliant idea: she's invited Jason to join them tonight. All evening she's been waiting for the right moment to tell her. The trouble is, there's never a right moment for news like that. Then she spots Jez.

He waves and shuffles over.

'Who's that?' asks podge-master.

Lauren, clearly bored with him too, says, 'Oh no, it's my fiancé.'

Jez lurches towards them in his grey mac. The podge-master looks round uncertainly.

'I just hope he hasn't brought his knife,' whispers Lauren.

The next time she turns round the podge-master has melted away.

Cathy had meant to be a little cool to Jez just to

show she noticed he went round to Lauren's first. But when she sees him, all she can think about is his beard. It looks like a stick-on. It's awful. You can't see his face at all now. He looks like someone you might find in Soho selling dirty videos. Really seedy. Not like Jez at all.

Jez lowers himself on to a chair. 'Cracking place, isn't it,' he says and then starts laughing.

Cathy suddenly realises how much she's missed that infectious laugh. Lauren gets up. 'Who wants a drink? Cathy?'

'No, I'm fine, thanks.'

'Jez? Or is that a silly question?'

Jez gives a waifish grin. 'Well a pint of Guinness would go down very nicely.'

'And what about Mark and Adam?' asks Cathy. 'I thought they would be here by now.'

'That's what I meant to tell you,' says Jez. 'They're still outside. Mark can't get past the Gestapo.'

Mark and Adam are in hiding round the side of the nightclub. 'You've got to go early, mate,' says Mark 'So you go on, I'll catch you up later.'

He almost wishes Adam would go on as it's really difficult keeping the optimism going.

'We'll get you in,' says Adam and in his best Baldrick impression adds, 'we've just got to think of a cunning plan.'

'Perhaps I could sneak in under your hair,' says

Mark. Then he paces back and forth, kicking at the stones. Probably when he's thirty he'll still have people asking if he's got any I.D. He'll never catch up. His kicking becomes fiercer.

It wasn't so much being refused entry that so enraged Mark – he was used to that – it was the way the bodyguard, a gleaming tanned giant, had looked at him and then given just the tiniest flick of the wrist, as if he were removing a microbe of dirt from his jacket, before bellowing in a jolly green giant voice, 'Sorry, boy but if we let you in we'd have complaints.'

Everyone behind Mark heard him. In fact, anyone ten miles away and hard of hearing could have picked up that insult. And inside, way inside, Mark was spinning around furiously. He wanted to break something, sob his guts out and punch that moron of a bodyguard smack in the face so that all that was left of him was an explosion of blood.

But Mark didn't show his anger. Do that and you're lost. They've got something on you then. Instead he just smiled broadly and sauntered away. That smile hadn't left his face since. Then he spots one of the guys who beat him up after school then took photographs of him. That was years ago. But late at night, they can still flash through his head. Especially Bonehead and that guy, his deputy, Ian Saltmore. Perhaps because Saltmore had the kind of face that made you think he sold baby food. He looked such a good little boy when really . . . Mark felt a squeeze of pain inside him. Then he remembered, Jason used to call where they lived, 'The Street of the Dead'. 'Just remember Mark,' he said, 'they're only zombies; uncollected corpses . . .' That always helped. But uncollected corpses – provided they're suitably elongated – can of course, walk straight into Charades.

'That's Saltmore,' says Adam, the guy who . . . ?' 'Yes, that's him,' says Mark quietly.

'Bastard,' says Adam, more to himself than Mark. Then his voice rises. 'Look who it is. Hey, Jas, over here.'

It's impossible to miss Jason, as he's wearing a giant red sombrero. On anyone else, Mark thinks, that hat would look as phoney as Bruce Forsyth's hair but Jason, well he carries it off somehow.

'That hat,' Mark exclaims, 'it's wicked. Where did you get it?'

'Off this Mexican bandit,' says Jason. 'He left it to me in his will. I've just been cleaning the blood off it.' He sniffs, 'still a bit whiffy.'

'Still talking the same crap,' says Adam, grinning.

'That's right,' says Jason, grinning too. 'That bodyguard giving you grief.'

'Yeah, we can't get past him,' says Adam.

Mark is grateful for the 'we'.

'I'm not surprised, wearing something as ram-

71

pantly hideous as that,' says Jason, pulling Mark's jacket. 'Just what colour is that anyway?'

'Pastel vomit,' says Mark quickly. He had liked the jacket beforehand, now he says, 'I'm only wearing it for a bet.'

'Take it off,' growls Jason and immediately removes his studded leather jacket. 'And try this.'

'Really,' cries Mark. And even though the jacket is several sizes too big, it feels right on him. This is what he should be wearing. Definitely. He walks about in it. Impossible not to strut a little.

Then they slick his hair back and Adam is saying, 'keep a serious face Mark, don't laugh – and deep voice.'

'Hey look, the bodyguards have changed,' says Adam.

An older guy with an impressive-looking paunch is now inspecting the queue.

'This is our chance,' says Jason. 'I'll try and distract the muscle from Mothercare while you sneak past.'

'In that hat no problem,' says Adam.

Mark suddenly remembers something. 'Jas,' he says, 'we're here to meet Lauren by the way, for her birthday,' he giggles nervously. 'She's legal now.'

'I know,' says Jason. 'Cathy invited me too.'

'Oh right,' says Mark, trying not to look too stunned.

'Are you and Lauren . . . ?' begins Adam.

72

Jason pretends not to hear. 'Come on lads, we'd better go,' he says.

Jez leans forward. 'So I did come round and see you and if you want proof . . .'

'Oh no.'

'If you want proof, Cathy, your next-door neighbour saw me. I know she saw me because her nose leaned forward. I bet she sees through that nose so she can testify to the fact . . .'

'Jez, I didn't mean . . .'

'She can also verify that I was on your doorstep at exactly 10.30, which was nearly an hour before I turned up at Lauren's. All right, face-ache?'

'You think I'm awful, don't you?'

'Yes.' Jez looked as stern as he could before breaking into a grin.

'While you're thinking I'm awful, can I say something really horrible about your beard. Jez, darlin', it doesn't suit you at all.'

'Oh cheers, I'm really enjoying this conversation.'

'You want the truth, don't you? But then I hate beards. They're so messy. Men are always leaving bits of their food behind in them for a start. Shave it off Jez, please.'

'You're only jealous.'

Cathy half-smiles. 'Tell me Jez, did you grow a beard to hide your pain after you and Yvonne broke up?'

'No, because I hate shaving. It was no big deal about me and Yvonne,' he adds. 'It just ran its course, that's all.'

His voice brightens. 'Anyway, you've gone and changed too.'

'Have I?'

He nods. 'The last time I saw you, you were wearing a blue dress – I can see it now. And every time I read one of your letters, that's how I pictured you. But all the time you were doing the dirty on me and changing. And look at you now, all in black except for your little parka. And no make-up.'

'Just a little cruelty-free lipstick.'

'Still a vegetarian then?'

'No, I'm a vegan now.'

'What's that – a vegetarian on speed?'

'No, it means I can't eat butter, eggs, cheese.'

'Why?'

'Giving money to factory farming. Jez, do you know, calves are taken away from their mothers after eight weeks. It should be several months.'

'Aaah.'

'And the cows only get one hour's exercise a day.'

'More than I get.'

'And the battery hens are kept in those awful cages all their lives. No, it's not funny Jez, you should come to the meetings with Jason and me.'

'So Jason's really into all this too?'

'Oh yes. In fact, Jez, I've done something really

silly. Tonight I've invited . . .' She stops and shakes her head at Jez just as Lauren returns with the drinks.

'I bought drinks for Mark and Adam too. I'm just wondering how we're going to get Mark in.'

'It's all right, look,' cries Cathy.

Mark is bounding towards them like a puppy that's been let off its lead, the huge red tongues on his trainers flapping down the steps. Adam could easily overtake Mark but he doesn't, keeping just behind him all the way.

Mark claps his hands. 'Hey, yes, yes, this is all right, isn't it?'

He gazes at the bar above them, then at the disco down below. 'They've really done this place up, haven't they?'

Cathy smiles to herself. Anyone would think he'd been here before. Two more huge, heavy chairs are placed around the table.

'That's it, squash round everyone,' says Jez, 'isn't this cosy.'

'Are these drinks for us?' cries Mark. 'Oh cheers, Lauren, happy birthday. We should be buying you the drinks. You look very nice, by the way.'

Lauren gives one of her long, lazy smiles. 'So do you.' Then she starts running her hands through Mark's hair. 'And look at all that gel. A girl's hand could get lost for a week in there.' She laughs wickedly.

'What's on your hair, Adam?'

'Just pure grease,' he says.

'And Mark, I love your blue jacket, but isn't it just a bit large?' Mark grins. 'It's not mine, it's Jason's. He's coming by the way. He just saw someone that he . . .' his voice trails away. Why is Lauren staring at him as if he's just punched her in the throat.

'He says he was invited,' he whispers. Actually he didn't quite say that but Mark's getting confused. He looks across at Adam for support. Lauren's voice is even fainter. 'Who invited him, on tonight of all nights?'

'I did,' says Cathy, feeling as if she's just confessed to murder. 'I decided it was time we all got together and that this silly feud was ended. After all, it's been almost a year, in fact, exactly a year now.' She realises she's adopting the tone her mother used when talking about HIM moving in. She looks around at everyone else. She hopes she's not sweating. 'After all, we were friends, the best of friends, weren't we?' She turns to Jez, almost begging him to speak.

He comes to her aid. 'We are friends. Together we amount to something, don't we?'

Adam and Mark nod fervently. Lauren looks as if she's about to spontaneously combust. Perhaps that's why Adam decides to change the subject. 'Lauren, these are from Mark and me,' and hands her the chocolates. 'Sorry they're only in brown

76

paper. I thought I had some proper wrapping paper at home but . . .'

'That's all right,' says Lauren, opening the chocolates like someone in a trance. 'Thank you. I'll enjoy eating these,' she says. 'Anyone want one?'

'I'll sample them for you, if you like,' says Jez.

'And what time is your friend arriving, Cathy?' asks Lauren, her voice tight with anger.

'I'm not sure.' Cathy can't even look at her. She's let Lauren down, hasn't she?

There's a silence now, broken only by some enthusiastic chewing by Jez. And there's a heaviness in the air, too, the kind you can smell just before a thunderstorm.

Jason never walks, he glides. And Mark doubts if his feet are actually touching the ground. It's the walk of the greatest poseur this side of Neptune. And yet, Jason makes it look so easy, so natural. And even now, he approaches with his usual easy swagger. Then smiles, tips his sombrero at them and shakes hands with Jez without betraying the slightest discomfort. That's style, thinks Mark approvingly. Jason brings a chair over next to Jez and opposite Lauren.

3 *Spontaneous Combustion at Charades*

He is just inches away from Lauren now, his sombrero almost touching' her but their eyes never meet. Cathy squeezed Lauren's hand and can feel her trembling. Just how many mega-volts of anger are jolting through her? Lauren moves her hand away from Cathy. If only she doesn't get up and leave.

Jason, in contrast, has both arms splayed out. He'd seem totally relaxed if he weren't swinging his right leg from side to side.

'Come on folks, anyone can be serious,' says Jez and he starts telling some very funny and highly unlikely stories about his year in Berlin. Then he says with a smug laugh, 'while I'm asleep tomorrow I'll bet you'll be bricking it, waiting for Postman Pat.'

'My parents are bad enough when they get my

report,' says Adam. 'They sit down at he table, go through it all. So tomorrow . . .' he shivers.

'I've warned mine already that I'm going to do really badly,' says Mark. 'I said I guess I'm just not intelligent. That always gets them. My Mum was almost crying. So I reckon I should be all right.'

'When in doubt, just say it got lost in the post,' says Jason. 'Gives you time to prepare something.'

'What about you, Lauren?' asks Jez. 'You getting worried?'

Lauren just frowns and shrugs her shoulders. There's an awkward silence, until Jez says suddenly, 'Did I tell you I've got a job? And don't all look so amazed. I've been for two interviews this afternoon. The first one was at this factory, picking up plastic. I thought, that only needs half a brain, just my style. So I go along in my nice coat and I'm the only applicant but I still don't get the job.' Jez looks indignant then starts laughing. 'So then I go for this interview at Radleys with this little Scottish lady. And I'm going on their special training session next week. So that should be a crack.' And he starts laughing again as if he's said something really funny.

'You working in Radleys, this I'll have to see,' says Cathy.

'And will you be wearing those awful grey overalls?' asks Mark.

'With pride,' says Jez.

Soon everyone except Lauren is laughing.

79

'Jason, you still posing about in that sports shop?' asks Jez.

'Full-time now mate,' says Jason proudly.

'Be manager in twenty years, won't you?' snaps Lauren, 'Mr Prospects.'

Immediately she's spoken Lauren regrets it. She sounds so snidey, while he's sitting back there, all easy confidence and charm. She should get up and walk away. But if she does that'll mean he's won. He will win, of course. He always does.

Lauren's thoughts are interrupted by a new voice. 'So what are you doing, holding a seance, tap twice if there's anyone there, eh.' A large blubbery face, with a crew cut is laughing down at them. He is wearing a polo-neck jumper with zips on it and is carrying a basket of roses, the kind, which if you're lucky, might live for an hour after you've bought them.

'Now I'm not sure who's going out with who and I won't try and guess,' he releases a smile which never actually disturbs the rest of his face, 'but I know you'll want to buy your lady one of these beautiful roses. And they're yours for just three pounds each, can't say fairer than that, can I?'

His little black eyes dart around the table. They alight on Jason and Lauren. 'How about you sir, a rose for your lady.'

For the first time that evening, even Jason looks embarrassed. He shakes his head.

80

'Well, I don't know girls, looks like you're going out with some right Jews.'

Adam clutches his glass tightly. He wants to say, 'Actually I am a Jew.' He has in the past and then drunk in their discomfort. Often someone will say, 'But you don't look anything like a Jew' (which roughly translates as, but you don't have a big nose).

This guy though, will probably just start telling Jewish jokes. And besides, Adam has discovered, when you tell people you're a Jew they start acting as if that's all that needs to be said about you. 'Oh you're a Jew, well that's you pigeon-holed.' And it was as if he – Adam Rosen – just ceased to exist. For a second he's tempted to say, 'Yes, I'll buy one of your roses,' just to show that this guy hadn't got to him. But then he changes his mind and shakes his head at Jason. No, he doesn't want anyone to say anything. These days he prefers to be anonymous.

So no one says anything until Jason calls out, 'I'll buy one of your roses, mate. Got change for 10p?'

The rose-seller gives him an evil look but he gets the message.

'What a faggot,' calls Jason after him.

'Place is crawling with them,' says Mark. 'One of the posse that got me is here.'

'Where, where,' says Jason. Never has he felt more eager to sort out one of the old enemy. 'You

81

should have told me before, Mark,' he says. 'No one pushes any of my mates around.' He's on his feet now.

'No, no Jason, not tonight,' cries Cathy. 'Please.' Immediately he sits down again.

But Adam thinks, we've moved close together, now we really do look as if we're about to hold hands and start a seance. He stares across at Jason. Suddenly he's the one they look to again. The leader. And perhaps Jason realises this. For he starts saying, 'It's been a while since we've been all together like this. What, with Jez being away . . .' For the first time that evening he's not acting as if Lauren is invisible. He's looking right across at her. 'Happy birthday, Lauren,' he says, then grins.

'Happy birthday,' she repeats, only she sounds as if she is turning the words over before spitting them out. Then she gives a strange breathless laugh. A year ago he'd made her feel like nothing. And now he thinks he can just smile sweetly at her again and everything will be all right. What's really making her mad though is that for the past year she's hated Jason more than she's ever hated anyone. That was her one consolation. It was as if a great iron door now lay between them and never again could he sneak his way back into her affection. That door was slammed shut for good. Yet now, he only has to sit opposite her in that ridiculous hat for it to blow open again. It just isn't fair. She gives that strange laugh again. She's too choked up to say anything else. Then she looks up, a scruffy-haired guy in a well-worn brown cord jacket and jeans catches her eye.

'Excuse me,' she says, 'I've just seen someone I know.'

'Lauren, do you want me to . . .' begins Cathy.

'I think you've done enough, don't you,' snaps Lauren.

'Bye' she adds, which comes out more as a strangled sob.

Cathy watches Lauren, convinced she's going to walk out. But instead, she shimmies up to someone Cathy's never seen before.

'Who's that, Cathy?' asks Jez.

'I haven't a clue. Do you think I should follow her?'

'I'd leave her for a minute or two,' says Jez. 'Let her calm down.'

Jason stands up and at first Cathy thinks he's going to go after Lauren. But instead he says, 'Who's for another drink?'

Everyone shakes their head. 'Just me then,' says Jason. 'That's fine.'

Adam looks at his watch. 'And I should have been home ten minutes ago.'

'But you've only just got here,' exclaims Jez.

'Yeah, one large coke and I'm off home again. Great, isn't it. Cheers, everyone. Good to see you back, Jez.' He gets up. Mark gets up too. 'I will be back,' he adds.

Jez and Cathy sit staring at each other.

'All in all,' says Jez, 'I should say this evening has gone down like a French kiss at a family reunion.'

Lauren beams one of her ripest smiles at the guy in the nondescript brown jacket and jeans.

'It's very crowded, isn't it?'

'It's all relative,' he says. 'To some people this probably isn't crowded at all.'

'That's true,' she says.

He's got a very husky voice. She rather likes it. She likes his age even more. He must be at least twenty-five.

'I suppose I ought to offer to buy you a drink,' he says.

'Yes you ought,' says Lauren.

They're both smiling now.

It's her mountain of red hair Mark notices first. She must be wearing a gallon of hair spray to keep it all puffed out like that. He imagines how difficult it must be manoeuvring that great juggernaut of a hairstyle through doorways. It really is over the top. She could be a time traveller from a dinner party of two centuries ago if it weren't for her denim shorts and seductive black tights.

Beneath that hair style is really quite an attractive face, with very green eyes and small, rather pouty lips. She's perched right at the end of the bar and keeps looking in her bag for something. Mark considers her more carefully. She's probably a noisy kisser. And passionate. Very passionate. She'd probably just lunge herself at you and cry, 'Take me to paradise, Mark.' Then she'd slowly unbutton your shirt, while rubbing her hand across your back – and oh yes – what a soft hand she's got. And then her hand would journey downwards . . .

He looks across at her again, gratefully. And then he freezes. She's smiling right back at him. At least he thinks it's him. It could of course be someone over his shoulder. It usually is. Or maybe she's just smiling about life in general. No, that was a high-voltage 'come over' smile and aimed at him, wasn't it? But then he thought about that girl in Radleys – enough about her. Stop thinking about your failures, concentrate on your successes. What successes? Well, he was the first guy in his class to have a wet dream. He was soaked, in fact. But after that early triumph – he knows nothing about girls. That's the truth. And that's why he wants advice. Adam, mate, where are you when you're needed. There's a girl here on my twelve o'clock, he could signal to Jas, who's still in the corner with Cathy and Jez. But if a viking-like Jason comes over, well, she'll stop smiling – indeed looking at – Mark for certain.

He edges towards her. She's riffling through her handbag again. Then he stops. What's he going to say? What he needs is a good opening line. But then Jason says there's no such thing as a good opening line, they're all corny. He reckons the secret is to remember that underneath, we're all just dying to have a really good laugh. So Jason'll just stroll up to a girl and he'll say something like, 'Excuse me, what's your name?' and she'll tell him, looking rather startled. Then he'll say, 'In my dreams I could only call you darling,' then he'll smile like crazy as if he's inviting her to share a joke and pretty soon she's laughing too.

If only he had the guts to try something like that. But he hasn't. Yet, he can go up and ask her questions, get her talking. Even he could do that. And anyway, what's he got to lose. So what if she's not interested. It's no big deal. He'll just hide away for the rest of his life, that's all.

He hunches up his shoulders, straightens up Jason's jacket and knowing he's wearing that gives him a swig of confidence, then plunges forward, just as she's joined by another girl. The extra girl is holding up keys and she's saying, 'But I don't remember leaving them there at all' and they're both chortling away so loudly they miss Mark's first cough.

He coughs again. 'Hello,' he says.

The girl looks directly at him, 'Hi.'

'My name's Mark by the way,' and his toes curl up with embarrassment as he speaks. For his voice has gone all soft and yukky, like hot toffee. He wouldn't blame her if she threw up all over him.

'I'm Becky and this is my friend Julie.' It's a

friendly, easy voice. The voice of someone who's quite chatty.

'And we've got to be going,' snaps Julie.

He ignores this. She's just an irritating blur in fact. Now she's found the keys he doesn't know why she doesn't push off and leave them.

'I don't think I've seen you here before, Becky,' he says. Keep repeating their name, Jason told him that. And funnily enough, Becky's a name he's always liked.

'No, I only moved here yesterday.'

'Really,' he edges a little closer.

'Are you a regular here then?'

'Well, I like to go clubbing in London best but they've just done this place up, so I thought I'd come along and see if they've improved it.' He stops. His voice still isn't behaving right.

'It's still a dump,' pronounces the blur.

'Oh yes, right,' says Mark. 'Seen more action on a bird-table.'

Mark starts to laugh, but as no one joins in, the laugh rapidly becomes a cough.

'And we've really got to go,' says the blur.

Rather more gently, Becky adds. 'Julie's come up from Bristol – that's where I used to live – to help me move in. And tomorrow morning we're off to Spain for two weeks.'

'*Early* tomorrow morning,' declares the blur.

'Last fling before I start college,' says Becky.

'Cartford College?' asks Mark.

'That's right, English, French and History "A" Level.'

'But I'm starting English and History "A" Level too.' The words are rushing out, but Mark's past caring now.

'Oh that's great,' and she looks really pleased. 'At least I'll know one person there. I was dreading just walking in and not knowing where to go . . .'

'Don't worry. I'll look after you, Becky,' says Mark, but he's not sure if she heard. The blur is pulling Becky away and muttering something about leaving at four in the morning.

'I'll see you on the first day of term, then, Mark,' calls Becky.

'Yeah and have a great holiday in Spain, Becky.' Mark yells after her.

She smiles, waves and disappears.

But long after she's gone Mark is still there, still drinking in the glory of what happened. To think, a most attractive girl − it won't take long to sort her hair out − had not only chatted and laughed with him but every time she'd looked at Mark he was certain, well practically certain, he'd seen deep fancying in her eyes.

Finally Cathy goes over. Lauren's been talking to that guy for over an hour. Just what is she playing at. He's not her type at all.

'Hi, Lauren, how are you doing,' she asks, fully expecting Lauren to freeze her out. But instead,

88

Lauren cries, 'Oh great, I was wondering when you'd come over. Grant, this is my very good friend, Cathy.'

They exchange limp handshakes.

He's wearing John Lennon glasses and peers at Cathy in a rather odd way, she thinks. Somehow, he holds his stares a bit too long. And he has the air of someone with a permanent sneer on his mind.

'Cathy, guess what,' cries Lauren, 'Grant can get us into Lombards.' Then, because Cathy doesn't look excited enough, she adds, 'You know Lombards, *the* nightclub.'

'Oh right,' says Cathy.

'Such excitement,' drawls Grant, 'I'm truly underwhelmed.'

'No, it's just,' Cathy looks at her watch. 'Oh yes, it's nearly eleven o'clock already.'

'Grant, will you excuse us a moment,' says Lauren.

She and Cathy go into a huddle a few feet away. 'First of all Lauren, I want to say I'm sorry about tonight,' says Cathy. 'I hadn't meant . . .'

Lauren waves her comments away. 'I know it's not your fault. You meant tonight for the best. It's Jason I blame, he talked you into this, didn't he?'

Cathy nods – that didn't seem quite as much as lying. She still feels distinctly feeble though. Why doesn't she own up. Because not saying anything makes life a lot easier, that's why.

'But Cathy, I really, really want to go to Lombards with Grant.'

'Why?'

'Oh I don't know Cath. I just feel like a little adventure, that's all,' and she starts giggling like a six-year-old at her first party. Cathy has a feeling she's drunk quite a lot in the last hour.

'So will you come to Lombards with us?' asks Lauren.

Cathy isn't impressed by Lombards. It's nothing but a poseur's paradise – just where she could imagine Grant. Except, he doesn't look anywhere near smart enough. Perhaps he'll get turned away at the door. Now that would be worth seeing. If her mum wasn't picking her up – well in exactly eight minutes . . . Her mum is always punctual. And so is Cathy. Tonight though, *he'll* be there too. So there'll be no cosy mugs of tea in the kitchen. Instead she'll just be trapped in her bedroom worrying about her exam results which are getting closer and closer.

'Oh, Cathy, please, please,' pleads Lauren. 'I'll go anyway,' she adds. And suddenly Cathy knows she can't let her go alone. There's just something about that guy . . .

'Oh all right,' she sighs.

Lauren claps her hands excitedly. She's growing younger by the minute.

'I'll just go and tell the others what we're doing,' says Cathy.

Lauren stops getting younger. 'Jason still there?'

'Yes.'

'See you outside then. Say goodbye to Jez and Mark for me. I'll ring Jez tomorrow.'

She makes as if to leave, then turns round again. 'Did I tell you he's twenty-eight and so intellectual,' she half swoons. 'Give me a proper man over a schoolboy any day, eh Cath.'

Cathy smiles faintly and longs to say – who are you kidding?

Grant's car gives a sudden cough, rather as an elderly seal might and stops yet again. The sound is beginning to irritate Cathy, as is the way he keeps whispering things they can hardly hear at the back. He half turns his head, 'Battery can't have gone flat on me again – I'll keep trying. You two all right?'

'Yes. We just want to go to a rave, that's all' cries Lauren. He mutters something in reply that Cathy can't hear. She's feeling distinctly uneasy, and she's not sure why. There's just something about him she doesn't like.

Then Grant starts muttering again. She nudges Lauren. His voice rises, though it's still little more than a whisper, 'Come on, come on,' he says. But the Volkswagen refuses to come to life. 'All right then . . . all right,' he sounds as if he is speaking through clenched teeth. 'You two, get out, go home, the evening's off.' And before they can respond he jumps out of the car and slams the door shut with such force the whole car shakes. Then he starts kicking the wheels.

'Right that's it,' says Cathy as they stumble out of the car.

He continues to kick at his car wheels with alarming force while they start walking away.

'I told you he was funny,' whispers Cathy.

Lauren doesn't answer. But she's holding on tightly to Cathy's hand. Then he must have noticed them moving away, for he starts calling after them. 'Keep going,' says Cathy. But then he starts running.

'Hey, hey, wait a minute,' he gasps, breathing heavily. He's clearly not very fit. For some reason this relaxes Cathy a little.

'Look I'm sorry – okay,' he calls. 'But sometimes life is just one long chain of frustration and you have to – but I only ever take it out on inanimate objects, all right?'

They both just stare at him. His tone becomes businesslike but he's still panting slightly. 'I'm going to have to ring for help. I'll get you both a taxi, that would seem to be the best thing to do wouldn't it?' He's trying to be helpful now and he's clearly deeply embarrassed. But Cathy is still suspicious of him.

'We're walking, thanks,' she says.

Lauren, standing beside her, doesn't argue.

'We don't live far away,' Cathy adds. 'In fact,

my family is probably out looking for me now. Come on Lauren.'

He steps forward as if he's going to ask Lauren for a dance. 'You shall go to Lombards, Lauren,' and he gives her a smile as if to say, I am really a right-on person. 'May I ring you?'

Lauren hesitates. 'Say no,' hisses Cathy.

Then he brings out his wallet. 'All right, you take my card. Ring me any time. I have an answering machine. So do it. Will you, please?'

'I might,' she says. There's just a hint of the old Lauren as she says it.

He smiles. 'You'd better ring me. Sorry if I scared you – put it down to my artistic temperament. See you again Lauren and – er,'

'Esmeralda,' snaps Cathy.

Why could no one remember her name tonight. 'And we're in a hurry.'

On the way home Lauren suddenly asks, 'Where are we going?'

'Home,' says Cathy. 'And how much have you had to drink?'

Lauren starts giggling. 'I don't know, he just kept getting me more and more drinks.'

'I bet he did, which is why I'm doing this.' She snatches the card out of Lauren's hand and tears it up into tiny pieces. 'Trust me, Lauren, that's one person you don't ever want to see again.'

At first Lauren doesn't think anyone's awake and

93

she starts to creep up the stairs. But then she hears a voice calling her from the lounge. Her father is sitting there in semi darkness with just one small lamp on behind him.

'What time is it, Lauren?' he asks.

'Eer – oh my goodness, it's just after twelve.'

'It's 12.34 and we made an agreement you and I.'

'Sorry.'

'So I'm afraid you owe me fifty pounds.'

She stares at him in amazement. Surely he hadn't been serious about that. 'Oh Dad, couldn't you let me off just this once? It is my birthday – or it was.'

He shakes his head gravely. 'A deal is a deal.' Then he gets up. 'I will accept a cheque,' he says.

4 Trailing the Dreaded Brown Envelope

Cathy had been sitting alone, except for Scampi, her amazingly spoilt spaniel who'd been snoring loudly at her feet since half-past six. She'd made herself a pot of tea. And now, nearly an hour later she's still drinking it. Of course, it's all cold and stewey now and disgustingly sweet, as she keeps adding huge teaspoons of sugar. But she doesn't care.

Then she hears the porch door open. She catches the post before it hits the mat. All the other letters are flung away as she tears open one solemn brown envelope. She stands there, staring in disbelief at the results, before slouching back to the kitchen.

They're not awful but they're not good. She's got Ds in English and History, the two subjects she wanted to do at 'A' Level. And she'd really worked for those two. It wasn't fair.

Upstairs she can hear muffled sounds. How he'll love this. As it was, he enjoyed himself last night. 'Your mother waited outside Charades one whole hour for you,' he said. 'I think your mother deserves an apology, don't you?'

And now she hears the stairs creak under his weight and he and her mum are giggling. They're always giggling these days. She slips the brown envelope down her jeans. Why should he be allowed to read that. It's personal. I'll tell them my results really quickly and then I'll say, 'I never want to talk about them again,' looking straight at him.

The kitchen door opens and Cathy heaps another teaspoon of sugar into her tea.

'You know you said if my results were better than you expected you'd buy me something,' says Mark.

'Did I say that,' says Mark's mum. 'Well, I must say your results were a very pleasant surprise. Your dad and I were fearing the worst. Go on then.'

'Well, last night Mum, my jacket got stolen.'

'Not your lovely coffee-coloured one?'

Mark shudders. 'Yeah, I just put it down for a minute – and then – gone. It ruined my evening I can tell you.'

His mum looks shocked, then adds, 'But I don't know if we can afford to buy you another one.'

'Well, if you could just give me something towards it and perhaps loan me the rest.'

Mark watches his mum carefully. She's starting

to weaken, he can sense it. Now all he's got to do is to stop her coming out to help him pick a new one. For he already knows exactly the jacket he wants.

Adam's face gives nothing away as he gazes at the results. Then he hands them to his father. His father puts down his toast and opens the envelope. Normally a faint smile curves itself around his father's lips. But today, his face is as blank as Adam's. Then, without a word he hands the envelope to Adam's mother. She wipes her hands before picking it up, then reads it and puts it down carefully. And still no one says anything. No one needs to.

Everyone is burning up with disappointment. Adam can almost hear it crackling away, eating deeper and deeper into his parents' faces. And part of Adam is angry with them for being so disappointed. They're quite respectable grades after all. There are no 'As' and only one 'B' but there's a cluster of 'Cs' – enough for him to take 'A' Levels at college. But light years away, of course, from his brother's results. His parents can't boast of his results the way they do about Reuben – 'And he gained all 'As' at 'A' level too, we were pleased; in his second year at Cambridge now and doing ever so well.'

His parents were intellectual snobs. Well, that was their problem, not his. But another part of

Adam shares their disappointment. He could have worked harder. He never really pushed himself. And of course, most of the time he said he was revising at Mark's – he was not.

'Are you pleased with your results Adam?' asks his mother suddenly. Here it comes, the inevitable *post-mortem*. But then the phone rings. It's his brother ringing up from Cambridge, to see how his little brother has got on. For Reuben realises how vitally important passing exams is. He revised non-stop for his 'A' Levels. How often has that fact been chanted. Adam also knows that Reuben will stick up for him. Whatever his results, Reuben will be positive about them. For Reuben's always been on his side, always looked out or him. Like the time when Adam's dad was shouting at him for having such a bad report. And he went on and on until Reuben stepped in crying, 'You're being too hard on him,' and straightaway his dad stopped and even tried being nice to Adam afterwards.

Right now, his mum's chatting away to Reuben as if she hasn't spoken to him in years and she's smiling and his dad's standing by the phone waiting impatiently to talk. Somehow, Adam can't imagine them ever talking to him like that. And why should they, they ought to like Reuben more than him. For all the respect his parents give Reuben, he's earned. While Adam has earned . . . No, between him and Reuben he deserves nothing. He knows that.

His father returns from the phone. His mother is talking to Reuben again now. He picks up his briefcase, 'We'll talk about this later, son,' he says. His tone is gentle, sympathetic even. This makes Adam feel even worse.

Debbie, Jason's younger sister, staggers down the stairs. She's overslept yet again. Then she stops. Is that Jason's voice coming from the lounge? Debbie tiptoes to the door, which is never usually shut, and does some earwigging. Yes, it is Jason on the phone to someone, only he sounds so different. Why is he talking in that posh, haw, haw accent. She bets he won't tell her. Everyone keeps their secrets in this family. He goes on, 'Oh, yes, I do understand the necessity for secrecy. Certainly,' he says, in that affected voice.

Then she hears him put the phone down. She edges open the door. 'What are you doing in here?'

Jason is almost dancing with excitement. 'I've only managed to find out where the bank holiday meet is, that's all.'

'You mean, he just told you.'

'Well I had to waffle a bit, drop a few names and do some pretty skilful acting.'

'And talk in that silly voice.'

'But it was worth it, Debbie, because now we know, we can be there too and we'll make sure no foxes get killed. Anyway, I've got lots to do now. See you around, Debs.'

99

'Oh, Debs,' he turns back. 'If you – no, it's all right.'

'No, go on, I hate it when people do that.'

'No, honestly, it's all right. No problem.'

As he goes rushing out of the door, Debbie notices a brown envelope on the kitchen table addressed to Jason. This must be his results. She decides to sneak a look. But he hasn't opened it. She gazes at the envelope in amazement. How can he not have opened it?

She runs to the door, waving the envelope at him. 'Jason, Jason, your results.'

He takes his headphones off. 'What did you say?'

'Your results. You haven't opened them.'

'No, too busy,' he says, walking away again. 'Lots to do.'

'But don't you want to know what you've got?' She's almost screaming at him now.

'To a man of my superior abilities they are utterly unimportant,' he calls. Then he puts his headphones back on and, whistling loudly, disappears.

Lauren watches the light gathering in the crack in her curtains. She hasn't been asleep tonight. She hasn't tossed or turned either. She's just been lying here while the same thoughts keep swirling around in her head. She feels dizzy and slightly sick now and not the slightest bit tired.

But then suddenly she does somehow slip away

while the light begins its full-scale assault on her room.

She jumps awake. She hasn't any clocks in her room. Their demented, never-ending ticking keeps her awake. But the light feels heavy, solid. It's late, isn't it? She twists her arm round and stares at her watch disbelievingly. It's ten-past twelve. Then, last night comes flooding back. Or the Jason part of it does, followed by her dad making her write that cheque. He won't really make her cash it, will he?'

Then she hears something. Did the stairs just creak? Is her Mum hovering. And then she sees it, waiting for her on the bedside cabinet.

She snatches it up. How could she have forgotten. She turns it over and sees it's already been opened. How dare they! Her mother's in the doorway, holding a red rose. 'Well done, dear. Your father and I are very pleased.'

'You had no right opening it.' cries Lauren. Then she sees her results – An 'A' in English and in Geography and three 'Bs' and ...

'Your father didn't want to wake you up as you were in so late last night.'

'You might have waited,' murmurs Lauren, too amazed at her results to be angry as she feels she should be.

'You father couldn't wait,' says her mum, smiling at the idea.

'And this is also for you.' She hands Lauren the rose.

'Oh thank you, Mum,' says Lauren.

'It's not from us,' says her mum. 'There is a card, which I didn't open,' she adds virtuously.

Lauren tears open the card. There is just one word on it in huge capitals, SORRY.

'From anyone nice, dear?' asks her Mum.

Lauren doesn't answer.

5 Conjuring Trick in a Supermarket

Cathy smashes down on her alarm button. It's half-past seven on a bank holiday and she's off to work at Radleys. Is there a worse way of spending a bank holiday? She hears whistling coming from the kitchen. Yes, watching him play cricket.

It's all because of him she's working at Radleys. She'll never forget the patronising way he said, 'But not all of us are cut out to be academics and though we'll be happy to sponsor you at college, money is tight.' And what was all this 'we' business. Just because he shared my mum's bed didn't mean he'd suddenly become my father.

Mum did say there was no question of Cathy getting a job if she didn't want one and she wanted Cathy to go to college. But the damage had been done. Cathy was determined to be independent, to fund herself at college. And now she can.

Radleys are putting her on the till again today.

It is supposed to be a compliment. It's just so boring.

She thinks enviously of Lauren.

She'll be asleep for hours yet. And when she does awake – will there be another rose waiting for her – with another one word message, SORRY. There've been two now, there's bound to be a third. And why won't she ring Jason? She knows it's him. It's got to be. Not that she can ring Jason today. He's out sabbing. That's what she should be doing, something really worthwhile. Still, at least Jez will be at Radley's too. She doesn't think she could bear today without him. She trudges wearily downstairs. She's almost tempted not to go into the kitchen because Giles is there. But then she thinks she's letting him drive her out, which she knows is what he wants, anyway.

She opens the kitchen door and for a moment thinks she's going to throw up, as the stench of fat floods her nostrils. She stares at him, gobbling down a huge plateful of bacon and egg, then she stares at the grill. 'Oh no,' she cries. 'You've left fat all over the grill.

'Someone's in a bad mood,' he says, with a smug smile.

'Who wouldn't be,' says Cathy, 'with that smell.'

She opens the window as wide as it can go and then starts to scrub the grill clean.

'If in future you'd be decent enough to wash the grill after yourself, I'd be most grateful,' she says.

He just shakes his head as if to say, what a nutter.

She's still working on the grill when her mum comes in. 'He's left fat all over the grill,' cries Cathy at once, almost begging her mum to take her side.

For the first time since Cathy came in, Giles stops chewing. 'And if I want to have bacon every day of the week I will. I'll have what I like and you eat what you like, just don't force your views on others. I like choice.'

'So does the pig,' snaps Cathy. 'And how would you like to come in here and find a dog had been fried on the cooker?'

'That's not the same thing at all,' says Giles.

'Yes it is,' says Cathy. 'Pigs are actually more intelligent than dogs.' Then as Scampi looks up reproachfully, she adds, 'Well most dogs.'

Cathy's mum half raises her hand. 'Giles darling, in future if you want to grill bacon would you mind just putting tinfoil over the grill and cook the bacon on top of it, that way none gets left on the grill, as it does upset Cathy.'

'And not just me either,' cries Cathy. 'Many other people . . .'

'Yes, yes, certainly,' agrees her mum. 'I'll finish cleaning up here while you have your cereal. All right dear?'

Her mum is being so reasonable. As always. She wants to be reasonable too. And if he weren't here she would be. But instead she picks up the cereal dish and says, 'I don't want dead pig near my food.' As she's walking out she sees Katie coming down the stairs. 'Katie' she whispers, 'when you go into the kitchen ask what that dreadful smell is.'

Katie obliges, almost screeching, 'Oh what's that awful smell?' while Cathy smothers a giggle. But later, when she goes back into the kitchen to say goodbye, her mum and him are rolling about laughing at one of his cricket stories. At once Cathy feels excluded, even though her mum says, 'What a pity you can't come with us today.' Mum's wearing this awful green dress he bought her. She looks as if she's in a pantomime playing an elf or something.

'And watch me hit a century,' he says.

Her mum laughs while Cathy gives a thin smile. She has a sudden urge to hug her mum very hard and yell, 'And you leave my mum alone. We don't want you.'

Cathy and her mum have always been really close. Perhaps her dad's sudden death – he just collapsed in a photographic shop while waiting to buy a new camera – made them more like, if not sisters, certainly allies. They'd spend hours talking together, putting the world to rights. Cathy remembered once being round Jason's house and his mum coming in and saying, 'Bye, Jason , see you in two weeks then,' as if she was just going down the shops. Jason barely looked up, too. And Cathy had been really shocked. For she and her mum could never have parted for two weeks so lightly. But then they have a special relationship. Or should that be, had a special relationship. It's slipping away now, isn't it? More and more things are being left unsaid. Like now, Cathy just says, 'I'll be off then. Have a good day.'

'And remember what we discussed,' says her mum. 'If you find it's getting too much . . .'

'Yes, all right,' says Cathy. 'See you tonight.'

She's at the kitchen door when he calls, 'And I hope no one wants to buy any bacon, or they'll be for it, won't they?' Then he gives a 'You're so weird' laugh, while Cathy just glares at him.

Jason lowers his scarf. The air is light and fresh on his face. He glances back at the other sabs clustered round the van before taking a few steps further into the field. He peers ahead of him. For as far as he can see there's nothing but hazy, white sky. Yet somewhere just beyond the horizon, he strains forward, are they really there?'

Jason's dressed like the other sabs – black jumper, combat jacket, jeans, army surplus boots – but Jason is also sporting a very distinctive red scarf with black skulls all over it. The scarf has been carefully arranged so that the one black skull is directly under his chin. One sab had dared to have a go at him about that scarf. 'We're supposed to be inconspicuous,' he said, Jason just laughed. Jason inconspicuous? Impossible.

Then he hears something, doesn't he? Only it's so faint, so far away, he's not completely sure. Has he really heard a horn? Seconds later, though, he hears it again, louder this time. He signals eagerly to the other sabs. And Eddie, who's nineteen years old and without a hair on his head, immediately starts walking towards Jason. He is carrying a harmonica. 'I always knew this would come in useful one day,' he says. He begins playing, lingering over each note. It sounds strange, eerie, the wail of something not quite human. But these odd noises ensure the hounds run off in their direction. And it isn't long before everyone can hear the hounds baying and howling.

The sabs are on their feet now, alert, excited. Captain Andy moves into the centre, carefully spraying his hands with lemon. Anything to make the hounds lose the fox's scent. The lemon is passed round, the smell reminding Jason of his downstairs loo.

And then suddenly the hounds are bounding towards them, all barking at once. They are very friendly, leaping madly around the ten sabs who pat them vigorously, until a voice roars – 'Get your hands off those hounds.'

And all the sabs step back. What else can you do when thirty horses clatter into view. And though they look like show horses, they're much larger.

Jason has heard tales of sabs being trampled by these horses. He can believe it.

'You are trespassing on my land,' cries a man in a moleskin hat, his buttocks bulging determinedly out of tight, cream trousers. 'So get off my land now or I shall call the police and you will get a criminal record. Go on, move yourselves.' He starts waving his whip around and you can tell he loves sitting up there, towering over them, yelling orders.

Captain Andy stands beside his van. 'We're on a public footpath and you don't own that,' he says quietly.

'You'd be shocked by just how much I do own, boy.'

And with that, the wind suddenly picks up, sending all the trees rustling behind him.

'I suppose you own the wind too,' says Jason.

The sabs laugh derisively.

'Don't entertain them,' snaps a woman in a bowler hat. 'They're all hired, sixteen pounds a day and a packed lunch.'

Jason stares at her incredulously. How can she think this is to do with money. But she repeats her accusation. 'They're all just hired thugs.' She's wearing such heavy red make-up she reminds Jason of one of his sister's china dolls. The ones that are starting to crack a bit.

'And you might bring a little more credit to your cause if you were dressed rather better,' she continues, staring at the two girl sabs. A woman behind her nods in agreement, while opening a tin of little party sausages. She snatches one up on a prong fork and hands it to the girl beside her. The girl can't be more than about twelve or thirteen but she's dressed identically to her mother; little black riding hat, tweed jacket, leather boots, her hair all tied up in a little bun. So it's a real family outing then, thinks Jason.

And what a great game, a battle of wits between them and the fox. Only of course, the day before the game they make certain all the holes are blocked up, so the fox can't win. All it can do is keep running for its life until it's exhausted. And if it should find a hole somewhere, they just send their terriers down.

Suddenly, four nasty-looking guys step out of a Land Rover. The biggest of them is nick-named Rottweiler. His neck is bigger than most people's waists. You wouldn't want to mess with him. You wouldn't want to mess with any of them. They're the terrier men or the muscle of this jolly day out. They're the ones who will dig the fox out of its hole or hit it across the head with a spade before throwing it to the dogs to be, as they put it, 'broken up'.

Jason saw a photograph once of a fox after it had been broken up. It looked just like an oily rag, with only the odd little bits to tell it ever was an animal.

'I will tell you just once more,' cries the man in

the moleskin hat, 'you are breaking the law and I order you to take yourselves off my land now.'

None of the sabs say anything. Captain Andy had discovered this is what really riles them. They're not used to being ignored.

'Do you hear me? Get off my land,' he blusters, his buttocks seeming to puff up with anger.

'I am sure you've all got better thing to do than this,' cries the woman with the sausages, looking straight at the girls. 'Like your homework, for instance.' Her tone becomes confiding. 'You're going to get all messy – and for what – foxes are vermin you know.'

So label foxes as vermin and you can do what you like with them. Whatever you call them they feel pain just as we do. That's what's important. Jason longs to shout this out at her, at all of them. But what's the point? They are standing just inches away from each other. Yet, it's as if there's a huge brick wall between them. And no words can climb over that wall.

So the sabs continue just to stare ahead of them, their denims flapping in the wind. The horses jostle and snort with impatience. And the girl starts whipping her horse.

'Stop that,' says Jason, moving towards her.

'How dare you,' splutter at least half a dozen voices. Before they can say any more, the horse bucks, throwing the girl right off. Jason leads the cheering.

'You communists, you vermin,' cries the man in the moleskin hat, hatred bursting out of his every pore, 'Let's waste no more time on them.'

Then he motions the group to start moving on.

But Jason yells after them, 'You're the vermin. And you're not killing any foxes today. I'll make sure of that.'

'Look out everyone, I think it's a BOMB,' yells Jez, hurling a brown package at Cathy.

It lands straight on Cathy's lap, to the accompaniment of loud gasps. And the queue by Cathy's till vanishes faster than today's bargain buys.

'Then again, I could be wrong,' he adds quietly. He grins at Cathy, 'I thought you needed a break.'

'Your're so right,' she sighs and stretches. When she started, she had to watch this training film in which this girl – a really pathetic actress – had gushed on about the importance of ' smart, clean fingers'. Then you saw her on the till being all smiley and saying, 'let me help you with that', to every customer she saw. Well, Cathy had tried to be just as cheery, only she'd soon stopped seeing faces, just an endless stream of tins and packets. 'In less than an hour,' she told Jez, 'I've turned from a moderately intelligent person into a con-veyor belt – scan item for price, ring up, scan item for price, ring up – I'll be looking for your price in a minute.'

'Oh, I'm very cheap,' says Jez. 'Bargain of the century you might say.'

Over the intercom a hearty voice starts braying with excitement about today's best buys.

'And that voice,' says Cathy, 'rots your few remaining brain cells.'

'You haven't had to handle any meat yet?'

'NO, THANK GOODNESS. A few people have bought beefburgers but at least they were in a packet, so I just gave them a look but when someone turns up with meat in cellophane with the poor animals' blood just dripping off it,' she squirms, 'I don't know what I'll do.'

Still, at the moment no customer is anywhere near her and that's wonderful, even if she does feel a twinge of guilt for the other girls, some of whose queues are stretching down into the frozen foods section.

'I had a bit of an accident witn one of the trolleys today,' says Jez. Originally Jez had been stacking shelves and displaying! But after placing one yellow toilet roll right in the centre of a pyramid of six hundred white ones (Jez said he was being artistic) he was demoted to what he calls the potato-head's job: collecting up all the trolleys from outside. Right now though, Cathy envies him. At least he could move around and he didn't have to pick up the remains of slaughtered animals.

'What's happened?'

'Don't really know,' says Jez. 'But somehow, one of the trolleys is in the river now.

'Oh Jez,' she gives a squeal of pleasure. 'But you will be careful.'

Jez has already collected two warnings. He shrugs his shoulders. 'There are plenty more bad jobs about. It's only if you've got a good job you need to worry. And anyway, right now we're being filmed, you know.'

'We are?'

'Oh yeah, the manager sits up in his office with a load of tellies, filming us just like the police do at football matches.'

'Why?'

'To check we don't steal a bar of soap. Shall we give him a wave?'

Jez begins waving and calling, 'Hey, boss-man, how are you doing?'

'Jez, stop it, he'll see you,' says Cathy.

Jez's grin widens. 'I'm only being friendly.' Jez is about to start waving again when he seen Mr Lurie, the deputy manager, bearing down on them, Mr Lurie is stooped and elderly. One gust of wind could blow all his wispy white hair away. Two gusts would be enough to send him into orbit.

'You wouldn't believe he's only twenty-four, would you?' whispers Jez.

Cathy smothers a giggle, then turns away from him. 'I'm not looking at you.'

'Ah, Miss Adams, started your break early, have you?'

'Yes, I got confused with the time. Sorry, Mr Lurie.'

'Well, perhaps you could spare me a moment.'

Cathy jumps up.

'Close your till first.' Then he squints at Jez. 'One of our trolleys has been discovered in the river. I don't suppose you know anything about it?'

Jez gives his wide-eyed stare. 'I'm afraid not – but how distressing. I'll keep a sharp eye on the other trolleys for you,' he says, before winking at Cathy and disappearing.

But as Cathy follows Mr Lurie through the plastic see-through doors into the corridor, she can't help feeling anxious. What has she done?

Mr Lurie clears his throat, then says, 'Mr Fanshaw has asked me to have a word with you.'

Cathy's insides start lurching. She hasn't even seen Mr Fanshaw yet. So all she can imagine is this giant, all-seeing eye, reclining on a huge cushion in a room full of televisions.

'Mr Fanshaw noticed you arrived for work wearing dark tights, when you were specially asked to wear flesh-coloured ones.'

Cathy shudders. It is rather creepy to think of this Mr Fanshaw secretly studying her legs.

'He also noticed you were wearing shoes with buckles, when I'm afraid buckles aren't allowed.'

115

'I didn't think it would matter,' says Cathy, 'as I'm sitting down.'

'It's important to get these things right,' says Mr Lurie. 'He is also concerned about your bangles and no nail polish please, just subtle make-up . . .'

It's like being at school again. Everyone has to be the same. Not even the tiniest flare of individuality can be permitted. Cathy starts bristling with anger. Why is life so full of petty rules? Why are people always trying to keep you down?

'But he did ask me,' concludes Mr Lurie, 'to commend you on your cravat. Some of our more senior staff can't tie the cravat as it should be tied. But you grasped it right away.'

Cathy gazes with undisguised distaste at her beaming, red cravat. It's disgusting. As is the horrible white blouse she has to wear with the cotton collar.

But Mr Lurie, misinterpreting her tight-lipped silence, leans closer and says, 'Don't be too disheartened, Miss Adams, you are allowed to make a few mistakes, you know.'

A few mistakes. Cathy wants to tell him to stick his job. Jez is right. There are plenty more jobs as bad as this one. But then she pictures the scene at home when she says she's walked out.

And Giles'll be there, smirking and saying, 'Couldn't even hold down a lousy job then, Cathy.' NO, he won't say it but he'll think it. And she'll see him thinking it too. So she continues to just stare ahead of her. Mr Lurie leans even closer to her. 'Like to see a piece of magic?'

Cathy looks up, startled. What's he up to now? Still, best to humour him. 'Oh yes, great.'

He digs into his pocket and produces a packet of polos. He takes one out and puts it into his left hand. Then he closes both hands up into fists. 'The polo is in my left hand, isn't it, Cathy?' She nods. Then he rubs his hands together.

'Now tap the hand you think it's in, Cathy,' he said, his voice rising with excitement.

Cathy taps the left hand.

'Let's see,' he opens his left hand. 'No, it's not there, is it?' and he thrusts his hand right up to her. 'Let's try the right hand, shall we Cathy?'

She nods, bemused but fascinated. And there it is.

'Now, how did it get there, you're wondering.'

'Yes, I am,' cries Cathy, and as the smile on his face widens – she feels a sudden burst of sympathy for him. Perhaps he wanted to be a conjuror once. Perhaps when he's all alone in this little office he tries out new tricks.

'But you're not going to tell me, are you?' she says. 'Because that's magic, isn't it?'

He nods. A definite gleam in his eyes now.

She goes to the door.

'If you would remember what Mr Fanshaw said,' he mutters, his face withering back into its normal constipated look again.

'Yes, all right.' Then, because she's more convinced than ever that he's a frustrated conjuror, she adds, 'That was a good trick you showed me.'

What Cathy's been most dreading is here, just inches away from her. Its blood is gushing all over the cellophane. And if she picks it up she'll have blood all over her hands too.

She looks around for Jez. He would pick it up for her but he's nowhere to be seen. He's probably round the back of the car park having a secret smoke. Perhaps if she just closed her eyes, or maybe she could pretend to faint. She's feeling a bit dizzy anyhow. No, she's being silly. She knows what to do. She picks up two carrier bags and very carefully puts one on each hand. The customer – a youngish woman in jeans – is watching her in some astonishment.

'Sorry,' says Cathy, 'but I hate doing meat.' Then she picks the meat up the way you might an unexploded bomb. 'I really hate the blood,' she says.

'I don't eat a lot of meat myself,' says the woman guiltily.

'I gave up eating meat completely two and a half months ago,' says Cathy. 'Never felt better in my life.' She hands her the wrapped meat. 'And you know, meat is full of so many impurities. That's £3.95 please.'

'My cousin's a vegetarian,' says the woman.

'More and more people are,' says Cathy. 'And if you saw what happens in those slaughter houses,' she shakes her head.

'I know,' says the woman, flushing with embarrassment. 'The meat isn't for me. I've really been cutting down lately,' she adds, before fleeing.

Suddenly in her mind, Cathy can see hundreds of shoppers all stopping eating meat as a result of her. Why, she's in quite a unique position to – influence people here, isn't she? She leans across. And she shouldn't have kept this hidden under the counter either. How could she be so cowardly.

Her next customer puts down a joint of beef, then gapes in astonishment at Cathy's new badge. It says, 'MEAT IS MURDER'. Cathy smiles gravely at her. 'And who's the meat-eater in your family then?'

'It's no good Jason, we've lost contact. Must be the hills or something,' says Eddie.

Jason reluctantly puts the C.B. down.

'Some you win, some you lose,' continues Eddie philosophically.

Jason doesn't reply, just stares ahead, breathing hard.

'There'll be other foxes to save, won't there, Jason?'

Jason still says nothing, just continues staring across the river. The whole hunt is there and they've got a fox, or almost got one. It's trapped down a hole and they've blocked up all the other exits and put a sack over this one. The terrier-men are hovering excitedly, spades poised. If the fox doesn't fall into their trap soon, they'll dig it out or send the dogs down.

The dogs are already baying eagerly. They sense something is about to happen. The hunters are leaning back on their horses, drinking from little hip flasks and looking very pleased with themselves. And already there's a real air of celebration. If everyone suddenly put on paper hats, Jason wouldn't have been surprised. Nothing like a killing for setting the party going.

One of the terrier-men looks across and, upon seeing them, laughs derisively. Jason clenches his fists so hard his knuckles turn white.

'Face it mate,' says Eddie, 'there's nothing we can do, is there?'

He's right, of course, thinks Jason. They've lost contact with the other sabs. So there's just the two of them now against about thirty.

'No,' says Jason finally. 'There's nothing we can do.' But even as he speaks he starts unlacing his first boot.

'What are you doing?' cries Eddie.

Jason doesn't really know. All he knows is he's got to do something. He can't just watch. And he feels quite calm and cool about it. In fact, he feels oddly distant from what he's doing. It's as if part of him is watching as he hauls off his other boot and throws his scarf to Eddie. 'Guard that with your life,' he says, before sprinting down to the river.

Eddie calls after him, 'What're you doing. You're only going to get your head kicked in and what use is that?'

Jason doesn't reply. Hasn't time. He's already wading into the river and the squelchy noises he makes are oddly reassuring. He's on the move, going forward. Eddie's yelling something else but he's too far away to hear. And there's no turning back. The river's up to his knees now. As he draws near to the other side he sees he is being watched. They're all staring at him, amused, curious, contemptuous. Only the girl is actually glaring at him. This is her first hunt and she doesn't want Jason ruining her big moment, when the fox's tail is rubbed across her forehead and its blood trickles down her face. That's her initiation ceremony. Once she's been 'blooded' she's really one of them. A member of their gang. He half-laughs. What do they know about gangs. When the six of them were together in that hut, all looking out for each other, now that was a real gang. But these hunters, what are they? The Klu Klux Klan with posher accents.

He clambers out of the river, the wind gusting behind him. He wonders if one of them will say something but no one does. They obviously think he's come to reason, to plead, to beg. That's why Jason decides to do the opposite. He half closes

121

his eyes, takes a deep breath, then roars 'YOU BASTARDS. I'M GOING TO BEAT THE HELL OUT OF ALL OF YOU.' And the wind tears the words out of his mouth and hurls them towards the hunters, their mouths open a yard wide.

So Jason presses home his advantage yelling out every insult he knows and he knows a lot. And then he starts jumping about like a demented witch-doctor. And all the time he's doing this a part of him is urging, 'Act crazier, go on.' Some of the hounds are jumping about now and then suddenly the girl's horse rears up again. She lets out a cry and for a split second everyone's attention is on her. Jason see his chance and hurls himself in front of the hole.

There he sits, cross-legged, watching the anger scorching all their faces. The man in the moleskin hat is the first to recover his speech. 'We've had just about enough of your sort coming out here, inflicting your gutter language on us. There are ladies present, you know.' Then he points his whip at Jason as if beckoning him. 'Now, get off my land. You've wasted enough of our time.'

In reply, Jason takes the sack away from the hole. 'Hang on,' he whispers both to himself and the fox. The whole hunt edges furiously around him. 'We'll just have to come out next week when this boy's at school,' cries an indignant voice. Rottweiler looms in front of him, holding a spade under his shoulder as if it's a rifle. 'If you don't move boy, I'm going to take your head off.'

Jason can feel a chill forming on his upper lip – the most cowardly part of his anatomy. For he'd heard stories of this guy attacking sabs before. Didn't he throw a sab down a hillside once? And a girl, too.

'You have five seconds to move or I'll move you.' Rottweiler starts counting. 'ONE ... TWO ... THREE ...'

That chill's invading Jason's lower lip now. He really doesn't like the way Rottweiler's waving that spade about. But all these respectable citizens won't let this madman attack him, will they? He gazes around him. Their faces display as much concern for him as a box of chisels.

'FOUR ...' a longer pause. Just don't let him touch my face thinks Jason. Anything but my face.

'FIVE.'

'FIVE.'

The word echoes around Jason like a gunshot. Rottweiler leans heavily on his spade. 'If you won't get out of our way, I'll move you.'

'You touch me and you'll get it,' cries Jason desperately, wishing he'd spent longer at those karate classes.

The Rottweiler's lank hair shakes with laughter. 'All right, you asked for it boy,' he murmurs.

123

Jason's breathing in gasps now and his face froze up totally some time ago. But he won't move. Can't.

Rottweiler clamps his teeth tightly. Any second now he'll strike. But instead he stops, turns his head, listening. Then Jason hears it too. A series of cries coming not from the hunt – but the river. And then he sees a small army of sabs striding towards them, waving their sticks in the air, as if to say, we're armed and ready to do battle.

'All right then,' calls Jason, hoping the sabs can hear him.

'I'll take the lot of you on. Now who's first?' But Rottweiler is already lumbering back to the hunt following a call from the man in the moleskin hat. Although these eminent citizens are happy for one sab to be kicked in, a pitched battle is more than these sportsmen can take. So as the sabs march towards them they're already preparing to leave. 'Ignore them, look the other way,' cries the woman in the black hat. And the hunters follow her instructions and seem not even to hear the sabs' cheers or Jason yelling, 'I told you, you wouldn't kill any foxes today.'

The sabs cluster round Jason.

'I tried to tell you I'd made contact,' says Eddie.

'Never heard you,' says Jason. 'Got my scarf?' he adds.

'But you must have had a real nut-out to think you could stop them on your own,' exclaims Captain Andy. 'Those terrier-men could have put you in hospital. What were you thinking of?'

Jason didn't know. But then, he didn't exactly sit down with a notebook and figure out what he should do next.

'I just had to do something,' he says. and it really was as simple as that.

He remembered the time he'd heard about Mark getting beaten up. And it was such totally unfair nastiness, that Jason knew his head would explode into a million steaming hot pieces if he didn't do something now. And they all thought he was such a hero when he'd do something crazy like sneak into Bonehead's house for those photos of Mark.

But he wasn't a hero, not really. He was more like this dog that Jason saw once, tearing around the village with this foam pouring out of its mouth. And everyone was rushing into their houses saying what an evil dog and it should be put down. Only Jason felt sorry for the dog. He even tried to catch it. For that dog wasn't evil. It just didn't know what it was doing any more.

And neither did Jason when he was 'being brave'. Act while your head's pounding away – and think about what you've done afterwards. That was Jason's philosophy.

And so often that philosophy worked like a charm. Cathy had said to him once, 'I always feel safe when you're around – whatever happens you'll come charging to the rescue. You're like a knight on a white charger.'

He'd glowed for weeks, no, years after that. The knight on a white charger, righting all the world's wrongs, that's Jason. Or it was. He'd tumbled right off that white charger at Lauren's fifteenth birthday. Never been able to get up again. He has tried. Once or twice he nearly rang Cathy. He thought at least she might understand. But some days even he doesn't understand why he did it. If only he'd . . . but he didn't.

Funny how it's only now he notices the half a ton of mud on his legs. He stumbles about, suddenly quite heavy with tiredness. But he's happy too. And it isn't because everyone – even Captain Andy is patting him on the back, enjoyable though that is. It's because so much of his life is just one pile of confusion. But out here everything becomes so simple, so clear. All that matters is saving a life. And the fox is saved, free.

'FREE,' he yells triumphantly, punching the air with his fist.

6 Welcome to Cartford College

'Now I suppose I ought to say a word about AIDS.' The head of humanities gazes around the rows of new students. 'Well I've only one thing to say to you about AIDS – don't get it.' He pauses, perhaps waiting for a laugh. But the only answering noise is the hall door creaking open as yet another latecomer stumbles over to the empty seat beside Mark, who yet again hisses, 'I'm sorry but this seat is reserved.' And each time he says it a little more forcefully, as if to convince himself Becky really is turning up. Cathy and Lauren, who are sitting on his other side, keep giving him sympathetic looks. They think he's made her up, don't they. Perhaps he has. Perhaps he's so girl-starved he's starting to hallucinate. After all, no one else saw her.

'And anyone caught supplying or buying drugs will be taken down to the police station.' The head of humanities gives another of his dramatic pauses. His grey hair, Cathy reflects, looks about twenty years older than his round, rather boyish-looking face. She suspects he's as wet as the Pacific Ocean.

But then she forgets all about him as the hall door flings open and Mark turns round yet again. Only this time he's waving his hand. Cathy twists round, too, nudging Lauren. The girl Mark's waving at is staring at him in some puzzlement. Oh don't say she doesn't remember him, thinks Cathy. But then the girl smiles – quite a bubbly smile, too – and hurries over.

'That's her,' cries Mark. 'Didn't recognise me at first in my glasses.'

Cathy nearly didn't recognise Mark either in his new Jasonesque jacket and round glasses.

'Hi, Becky, great to see you. How are you?' he cries, totally unaware of the glare he's receiving from the head of humanities.

She falls into her chair. 'This morning has been just mad. First I go over to the science block, then I come speeding over here, trip over the steps . . .'

'Oh no,' Mark winces.

'Still I'm here now,' she says. 'What have I missed?'

'Nothing,' says Mark. 'Becky, these are my very good friends Cathy and Lauren.' Shy smiles are exchanged. She's attractive, Cathy thinks, and her hair is spectacular. It's funny, Cathy can shove all these slides and clips into her hair but still it doesn't happen. Her hair just refuses to look glossy. 'She seems fun, doesn't she?' she whispers to Lauren.

Lauren just shrugs, 'We must tell Mark not to be too keen. It's offputting.' Cathy nods. She's the world's leading expert on being too keen – and too helpful. The trouble is, it's only afterwards you realise how embarrassing you've been. Still, it's great Mark has found someone who at least seems decent. He'll make a good boyfriend. She'd like Adam to get fixed up, too. He's in the other hall with the science students. But they're all meeting up at lunch-time. Jez is hoping to drop in too – and Jason.

This time, she'd told Lauren straight out that Jason would be around. Lauren had just received a third card saying SORRY only this one had a thousand Xs added underneath. There was another red rose, too. It was obvious that it was Jason. And Cathy has been quite blunt with Lauren. She'd said, 'He's apologised three times – how many more apologies do you want.'

And Lauren had replied, 'Oh Cathy, don't put it like that. And anyway, we don't even know it is Jason.'

'Of course it is Jason,' Cathy had cried, becoming quite exasperated with her.

But then, later that same evening Lauren suddenly said, 'About Jason, last year I swore I'd never let him hurt me again. And I really thought I had broken his spell.'

129

What an odd way of putting it, Cathy had thought. But thinking about it, she supposed being in love was a bit like being under someone's spell.

'But now,' Lauren had continued, 'I'm all confused – and afraid.'

She didn't say anything else, just sat twisting her hair until Cathy said, 'No one's asking you to go out with him again. Just talk to him or at least don't freeze him out. Would you do that?'

'I don't know.'

'Because you two not talking does make it really awkward for us. Lauren, please.'

Lauren stood up. 'Don't keep on at me Cath, I just don't know, all right?' And that was how they'd left it.

The rest of the lecturers are filing in now, to be introduced by the head of humanities, who makes a jokey comment about each one to the accompaniment of embarrassed smirks and laughs that sound more like burps. Still, at least it's better than her old school assemblies with the headmaster raging on about how thou shalt keep top buttons done up at all times. Cathy's eyes keep returning to all the ripped jeans, bangles, and chains all around her. What would Nut-out have done if they'd all turned up on the first day dressed like this. He'd have had a seizure at least, wouldn't he? She's just imagining this joyous scene when she receives the shock of her life. For the lecturer being introduced as the head of English, Mr Withers, is the guy who wanted to take Lauren to Lombards and started assaulting his car when it wouldn't start. What was his name?

'It's Grant,' announces Lauren.

'I know, what do you think?' says Cathy.

'I don't think he looks so good in a suit. He should only wear casual clothes.'

'No, I mean – about him teaching you – us.'

Lauren gives one of her wicked smiles. 'It should be fun,' she says.

Unlike the other lecturers, Grant doesn't titter at any of the head of humanities' puny jokes. He just stands there totally cool, self-possessed, not at all the sort of person you'd expect to attack his car. Lauren smiles again. That will be their little secret. Quite understandable of course. He was obviously just teeming with frustration at not being able to take her to Lombards. And a senior lecturer too. Lauren is feeling distinctly chuffed, when for an instant he looks right at her. And he doesn't seem at all surprised she's there. In fact, it's almost as if he'd expected her to be there. It's then she has another thought. What if it isn't Jason who's been sending her all these cards? BUT HIM!!

And suddenly, Lauren isn't smiling any more.

'Shall we take a peek into one of the classrooms?' asks Becky. She and Mark have sneaked away from the official college tour.

And before Mark can reply, Becky says, 'How

about the one with no glass in the door.' She turns the handle. 'It's not locked.' Then as she steps inside she adds, 'And I can see why.'

It's certainly, Mark thinks, a contrast to the deep carpets and plush furniture in the reception hall. Everything here is so shabby and dusty. It looks more like a disused waiting room than a classroom.

'After being in here you feel like you need a bath, don't you?' declares Becky, jumping on to the teacher's desk. 'And why are all the walls the colour of gunge. Why couldn't they have painted them blue or green.'

'Or purple with red spots,' says Mark, sliding close beside her. She laughs. 'Yeah, why not. Mark – listen.'

'What.'

'Exactly, total silence. You don't suppose we should be somewhere now, do you?'

Mark bends down and fishes out of his bag a brightly coloured pack headed, *Welcome to Cartford College.*

'Where did you get that?'

'From reception, there's a big pile of them just by the entrance.'

Becky sighs. 'And I missed that, too. Typical.'

'It's all right,' says Mark, 'I got one for you too, just in case . . .' He hands the pack to her. She stares at him, genuinely surprised and pleased.

'That's really nice of you. Thank you, Mark.'

He feels himself blushing with pleasure. 'The first sheet is the plan for today,' he says.

She skims this *Official Welcome*, had that, SNORE, SNORE, tour round the college, doing that. Next is, 'Listen to this,' she reads aloud. 'Free coffee and snacks will be served in the hall from 10.30.' She grins, 'Mustn't miss that, Mark.' Then she continues reading, 'Representatives from all the student groups will be there, so this is your chance to learn more about the drama, music, debating and sports activities in the college. Representatives from student pressure groups, like anti-racism, anti-sexism, animal rights . . . will be around.' She half-smiles, 'and advice and leaflets will also be available on safe sex!' She puts the pack away. 'Thanks again for getting me this, I was really dreading today you know. I mean, when my Mum dropped me off this morning I said, "It's no good. I can't walk in there. I can't." '

'What did your mum say?'

'She said, "Becky, sometimes we seem to spend our life walking through an endless line of burning doorways. I understand exactly how you're feeling." Then she pushed me out of the car. She's a writer, my mum. But you won't have heard of her,' she added. 'No one much has, yet.' She went on, 'And then I could hardly walk into that hall I was shaking so much, I really hated not knowing anyone. So when you waved to me it was such a brilliant surprise. I can't tell you how much I appreciated that.'

Mark tries to shrug his shoulders modestly. 'Didn't think you recognised me at first.'

'It was your glasses, made you look so intellectual.'

'You wouldn't believe it, Becky, but when you're wearing glasses, people see you totally differently. They listen to you more and they think you know what you're talking about. I reckon everyone feels a bit smaller if the person they're talking to is wearing glasses.'

'How strong are they?'

Mark hesitates for just a second, and then even though there's no one else in the room, lowers his voice. 'Don't tell anyone but they're just clear glass.' He grins shyly.

And she immediately smiles back, a wide, generous smile, and Mark thinks yes, you're the one. You're the girl I've been waiting for.

Outside there's a sudden stampede of voices.

'It sounds like everyone's rushing off for their free snacks,' says Becky, jumping down from the desk. 'Shall we go?'

They jostle their way down the corridor, Mark nodding at the occasional person from his old school. And then he sees Ian Saltmore. The guy looks at Mark without even a flicker of recognition. Mark was obviously just one of his many victims. But Mark remembers him all right, even though his face has thickened and he's got the beginnings of a beer belly. Even when that guy's seventy with a beer belly the size of ten balloons and with his one remaining strand of hair stretched over his skull Mark would recognise him. And hate him.

Mark starts walking faster. Don't think about him, think about your mates in the hall.

'When we get to the hall Becky, I'll introduce you to Adam, he's my best mate. You'll like him. He's a really interesting person to talk to.'

'How long have you known him?'

'Centuries. We were in a sort of gang together with Lauren and Cathy – whom you met. And Jez, he might be there too. He's a great crack. And Jason was like the leader – actually I don't know if I should introduce you to him.'

'Why?'

'Because once you see Jason you'll never look at me again,' says Mark laughing just a little too loudly. 'For when the girls see Jason . . . '

'Oh, I don't go for looks,' says Becky.

'You don't?'

'Well, actually I do but they've got to have a good personality as well.'

'He has that, too,' says Mark, a little sadly. 'Everyone wants to be in with him. I mean, dogs cross the street just to be patted by him . . .'

Becky starts laughing.

'The only problem is, he and Lauren went out together and then . . .' He stops and then sees why

Becky is nudging him. For staring at the timetables in front of the library is Lauren, pen in hand. Only she's not writing anything down.

'Lauren, hey, you all right?' cries Mark.

She whirls round. 'Hi Mark and er . . .'

'Becky,' prompt Mark and Becky together.

'Oh yes, sorry. Just writing out my timetable.' She glances down at her empty piece of paper. 'Well, I haven't started yet, you going to the hall?'

'That's right,' says Mark.

'Well, Cathy's down there all ready on the animal rights stall. Catch you up in a minute then.'

'Okay, Lauren, see you then,' Mark sensing she doesn't want to talk. Lauren feels a bit mean not chatting longer to Mark and for forgetting his girl-friend's name. But she's a bit preoccupied with something she's just done. Something very silly.

She'd just gone down into the hall, spied Jason talking to Cathy at the animal rights stall and immediately hurtled right back out of the hall faster than a loose cannon ball.

That's why she's pretending to examine this timetable. She needs time to think – and space. But there is no space. If only she could be invisible for a few minutes. What about the library? But of course. Surely she can sit quietly in there.

Inside a group of students are sitting reading the newspapers and chatting, obviously second-years. She recognises one of them from her school. Lauren certainly isn't in the mood for a cheery chat now. So she lowers her head and journeys over to the back of the library. Here no students lurk and the books are lined up so neatly and so tightly she knows no human hand has run along this shelf for aeons. If ever she wanted to hide a dead body this is where she'd haul it. No one would see it for months. Well, eventually the smell might alert them. She shakes her head, why is she speculating about that?

She wants to sink down into a chair – except these aren't the kind you sink into. So she sits up straight again. She's here to try and explain her highly immature and un-Lauren-like behaviour of a few minutes ago.

JASON. It's his fault. Jason – it had seemed so easy the night she'd stabbed his name out. Jason wiped off the pact, Jason wiped out of her life. And she really did want Jason out of her life. The only problem was, she also wanted him to try and contact her. That's what really hurt. In a year, he'd made only one miserable effort to talk to her – a thirty-second phone call.

So he'd obviously got over her (if he'd ever cared in the first place) while Lauren – who had got everything going for her (or so people said) – had never felt more miserable, and was reduced to sneaking looks at him in the sports shop where he worked. She'd skulk outside watching him talking and laughing until she couldn't bear the sharp, throbbing pain this scene gave her, any longer. Yet she kept returning for another draught of misery. Until, suddenly, she's the lucky recipient of all these cards and roses. But are they from Jason, that's the question. The boy who never once sent her a flower or a card. The boy who just despised Valentine's day. That's why she thought it might have been Cathy doing it, trying to bring them together.

But just when she'd grown more and more certain it was Jason, up pops another suspect. Grant. Did she tell him she was going to Cartford College? She thinks she did. So he could have got her address from the student records.

So maybe it was him? No, it must be Jason. Mustn't it? And if Jason sent her the cards then she'd be certain that he had suffered, too. She knows that sounds a bit warped and no one, not even Cathy, understands. But it's important to her.

She stands up. Well why doesn't she just ask him outright. She could say, 'Jason have you sent me three cards and roses – and then SHE'D KNOW. WOULDN'T SHE? That's what she must do.

She runs her hand excitedly along the spines of the aged texts in front of her until one of them coughs indignantly. She jumps back and then sees a woman in stripey black trousers staring at her.

'I'm the librarian. Are you looking for anything in particular?'

'No, it's all right,' says Lauren. 'I think I've found it.'

It's like walking into a party, thinks Adam, as he edges his way into the hall. That same tidal wave of noise, that same table of bowls of crisps and peanuts, though he doubts if any self-respecting party would have huge pots of coffee and tea as the only drinks.

And he feels too hot, just like he always does at parties. Only this time it's these evil germs inside him that are burning him up. And his throat feels so raw and he keeps sneezing which is a bit embarrassing when you haven't got a hankie to remove any nasal danglings.

He looks around uncertainly. At parties, Adam just does a quick turn around the lounge before settling on the stairs or in the kitchen, which is where most of the interesting things happen anyway. But here, there's nowhere off-centre where you can watch the action. You either join the scrum around the food or you brave the stalls where the student representatives hover like eager sales assistants, ready to pounce on anyone showing the tiniest glimmer of interest in their society. That's why Adam keeps his head down and deliberately avoids catching anyone's eye until he reaches the animal rights stall. There, a girl is returning a leaflet to Cathy with the words, 'I won't take it, thanks. It will upset me too much.'

Cathy gives a somewhat glazed smile, and then a much warmer one when she sees Adam.

'Cathy, you haven't got a spare hanky lurking somewhere, have you?'

'Yes, sure.' she pulls out one of the lace-edged variety. 'My mum picks them, I'm afraid.'

'No, that's fine, thanks a lot.'

'Are you suffering then?'

'I think I might be getting the flu.'

'You do look a bit flushed,' says Cathy, but in a way that rather suits you, she thinks. And even in that unflattering duffel coat, Adam can't help looking handsome. He may not have the heart-throb looks of Jason. But with his long, jet black hair and sensitive, open face, you could imagine him playing the guitar and singing sad songs about love and the ozone layer. She's convinced that while he's at college a girl will snap him up – someone gentle and sympathetic – but with a good sense of humour. In fact, if Cathy hadn't known him all these years she, herself might . . .

She realises Adam is talking to her and she's not heard a word. 'Sorry, I missed that.'

'You're lucky. No, I just said, you're doing quite a good trade here.'

'Well, not bad, quite a few have taken leaflets anyhow. Two other people are supposed to be on with me but they haven't turned up. In fact, I haven't seen anyone but Jason, who's over there being silly.'

She gestures towards Jason. He's sitting at the end of the animal rights enrolment desks and has his jersey pulled up, right over his head.

'What's he sitting like that for?'

Jason lowers the jersey down to his nose. 'Because she's giving me loads of hassle, mate, that's why,' and before Cathy can reply, the jersey is pulled back up again.

'Adam, all that happened was, I asked Jason if he'd· help me with this anti-meat demonstration I'm planning outside Radleys when the managing director's visiting. And Jason said he didn't do that sort of thing. And I said, well, yes I did have a bit of a go at him,' she leans forward . . . 'Adam you'll come on this demonstration with me, won't you?'

'Yeah. Okay. Sure.'

'Oh brilliant, Adam. Don't worry, I'll send you all the details,' she says, getting out a large piece of paper and writing his name down.

Adam peers across. 'I can't see any other names on the paper.' Cathy looks up, 'Yes, you're the first but don't worry, there'll be hundreds more.'

'Look, I'm disappearing to the chemist for a miracle cure now. Will you tell Mark I'm not feeling too good and I'll ring him . . .'

'But, Adam, you can't go. You haven't met Becky yet.'

Adam groans. 'How could I forget her. Mark's talked about no one else for weeks. Have you met her yet?'

'Only very briefly. She's attractive – and seems really lively. I liked her.'

'Oh good.' Adam looks pleased. 'Will you tell Mark I'll be back in about ten minutes.' He grins. 'And when are you going to put Jason out of his misery?'

Cathy looks across at Jason. A large audience of girls is now watching him. He really is such a show-off. And all she'd said was, he was more concerned with his image than animal rights. And that was true. He'll go on sabbing because that's he-man stuff. But anything like helping at jumble sales to raise money and going on demonstrations he won't do because . . . She looks across at him and finds herself softening. He just has to have his little cover. But then so do most other blokes.

Funny how he can be really brave like on that last sab hunt – and yet a bit of a coward too. But even as she's thinking this she's walking over to him and smiling. Hard not to when he's peeping out from under his jersey at you, like a timid squirrel. Then he mutters, 'All right. I'll come on your crappy demonstration.'

'Oh, Jason, thank you.'

He pulls the jersey down. 'Just don't give me any more hassle, all right.'

'No, Jason.'

'And I've put your name forward to go on the next sab in November. Don't know why, 'cause you'll only give me hassle.'

142

'Probably,' says Cathy, giving him a quick hug.

'But I'll look out for you,' he says, 'though you don't deserve it.'

'Jason you're so good to me,' but despite her sarky tone, she knows he will.

'It's just such a shame you won't be at college. Why won't you? Your exam results were okay, weren't they?'

'College is just a waste of time, for a man of action like me, that's why.' He looks around. 'What's happened to Adam?'

'He's not feeling too good. But he'll be back in a few minutes to meet Becky. We're all meeting then . . . Lauren as well,' she adds significantly, hoping for at least a beat of emotion on his face. But as usual he gives nothing away. And somehow, fond as she is of Jason, she feels she can't push it, not on something personal like that. For even when he's at his friendliest, there's still this barbed wire around him to stop you getting too close. And anyone daring to cut through that barbed wire would be scorched in seconds by those brilliant blue eyes.

'We'd like to join your animal rights group,' chorus three girls who've been poring over the leaflets.

'Oh great,' begins Cathy but then she sees they're staring right at Jason.

'I'll enrol these young ladies for you,' says a grinning Jason. He sits down at one of the empty

143

desks. 'Do please take a seat ladies,' he adds, in his most businesslike voice.

Cathy smothers a giggle and goes over to the main display just as Jez arrives.

'This is a bit of all right, isn't it,' says Jez. 'Free nuts and a pocket full of condoms.' Then Jez plonks a white carrier bag down,

'Look after this for me, will you.'

'Oh sure, got any laundry you'd like to leave, too. What's inside anyway?'

'Books, they're selling them off at 20p each over there. And I get through a couple of books a day out there on the car park you know.'

'You want to be careful,' says Cathy, putting the bag away. 'Yesterday I heard our esteemed deputy manager asking, "And where's Beardie – skiving again." '

'Beardie, is that what he calls me?' Jez sounds indignant.

'I expect he calls you far worse things in private.'

'Still, who's in trouble for wearing naughty badges then.'

'I don't care,' says Cathy. 'So many of the women I talk to don't know anything about the slaughter houses and what goes on there.'

'I bet Radleys' meat sales are going to be right down because of you.'

'Oh, I hope so,' says Cathy fervently.

And Jez wonders yet again how Cathy can

manage to seem so good and so absurd at the same time.

Cathy gets out her sheet of paper. 'Now I can put you down for the demonstration.'

'What demonstration?'

'The one I'm planning for outside Radleys when the managing director turns up. You've got that day off too – we checked.'

'Ah yes, but er – something's come up,' says Jez evasively.

'What?'

'I've got to mend my bicycle.'

'Why?'

'So I can ride it again.'

'I didn't know you had a bike.'

'No, well it's been broken for about three years. It's one of those black ones. What are they called? The penny-farthing.' He grins. 'I'm having real difficulty getting parts.'

Cathy smiles unwillingly. 'You can't be mending your bicycle all day.'

'Yes, but then I have to – tidy my sock drawer.'

'Why don't you just say you don't want to go on the demonstration.'

'All right. I don't want to go on the demon-stration.'

'Why?'

Jez looks up. 'Personally, I think it's a waste of time. I mean, what's it going to achieve?'

'Oh, Jez, what sort of attitude is that.'

145

'Mine.' He looks around and with some relief says, 'And look, here's Mark with that girl he's been going on about.'

'Becky,' says Cathy, adding 'and if you don't come on my demonstration I'll never talk to you again.'

'Can I have that in writing?' says Jez.

Lauren watches Mark introduce Becky to Jez. Now Mark and Jez are laughing at something Becky's said. She's certainly not shy. Then she watches Jason spring over to her. As always, he moves like a panther who's having a particularly good day. Lauren watches Jason and Becky shake hands as intently as any jealous girlfriend. Then she juts her chin out and says to herself, 'Here we go, then.'

Mark sees her first. He waves and she can feel an awful fixed smile forming on her face. Funny how in moments of stress she smiles just like her mum.

She doesn't remember walking those last few feet at all. She's just suddenly there and Cathy's saying, 'All right darlin'?' She nods and then Cathy says, 'So we're all here now except Adam.' Then she says something else about Adam which Lauren doesn't hear because Jason is now strolling away from the desk and the three girls. And as he approaches, she says 'Hello, Jason,' crisply, clearly, neutrally. And he immediately steps forward and says, 'Hello Lauren, how are you?' Only in such a serious, formal voice, her heart starts doing high jumps. He *does* care.

'Oh, I'm fine, how are you?' She could be talking to one of those relations you only see at weddings or funerals.

'Busy, really busy.' Every word has had its meaning worn away long ago. But he's smiling now and she can see that little gap between his two sparklingly white front teeth – his one glimmer of imperfection and he looks suddenly so young and so lost, that everything she wants to say dies somewhere in her throat. So they just stand smiling at each other while everyone else plays statues, only with faint grins on their faces as if they're waiting to have their photographs taken.

And the silence swells suffocatingly until finally Lauren says, 'See you around then,' and rushes off 'to get a coffee'. And Jason returns to his desk and the waiting girls. Only this time he doesn't look up and is writing very quickly.

'A thaw, a definite thaw, don't you think,' says Cathy to Jez.

'Yeah, but where do they go from here?'

'We get Jason to tell Lauren he's been sending her all those cards. You couldn't have a word with Jason, could you?'

To her surprise, Jez says, 'I rather think it's time I did.'

Mark and Becky have moved a little way off and Becky is exclaiming, 'I could tell there was something between them, just by the way they were looking at each other. And you say they haven't spoken to each other for a year?'

'Over a year now,' says Mark. Then he yells, 'At last, where've you been?'

Adam comes over, grinning sheepishly. 'I'm suffering, mate,' he says. 'I'm not a well man you know,' and because he feels a mess he doesn't look Becky in the face at first and mutters, 'Hello, pleased to meet you,' to her rather dappy green trainers.

Mark shakes his head fondly. Adam is so gauche with girls now, so clumsy. But then Adam does look up and Becky shakes hands with him, just like she had with Jason and Jez. Only this time it feels different. And it isn't just that she seems to linger over this handshake. It's the way her smile keeps expanding every time Adam looks at her. She's doing all this, Mark decides, because he's my best mate. He can't help feeling she's rather overdoing it, though.

7
Adam's Secret

'Look, mate, if you fancy her I'm not interested,' says Adam. He is sprawled across Mark's bed doodling half-heartedly. Mark is sitting by the window, washing his new light cone in disinfectant, saying nothing. 'And I mean that, mate,' says Adam. Mark still doesn't reply, apparently completely absorbed in his task. Then he says calmly, quietly, 'But she doesn't fancy me.' And there's another distinctly embarrassed silence.

Half the college think he and Becky are a couple. For they are always together and get on well, really well. Becky says no one can make her laugh like Mark. That's why he's awake half the night rehearsing funny stories for tomorrow. And he looks out for her, listens to her and showers her with little presents – and it isn't enough.

While Adam just has to smile at her in the corridor for a scratchy black and white day to explode

149

into rich technicolour. No wonder her eyes are suddenly dazzled and her pulse is racing. And how can Mark, trapped in bleary black and white, compete? He can't, of course.

So isn't it better to back away gracefully now, than risk pushing it with Becky only to hear her say in a tone of desperate sympathy, 'Oh, Mark, I like you so much as you're so funny and generous and helpful – but as a friend.' Sometimes Mark thinks they're the six cruellest words a girl can ever say to a boy – 'I like you as a friend'. For what she's really saying is you haven't an atom of sex appeal. You're something less than you should be. And he'd rather die – yes, literally die – than ever hear Becky tell him that. That's what she thinks, of course, but to actually hear her say that. No, NO. At least he can show some dignity, some style, and put the lid on it now.

'I just can't do it to you', says Adam. Poor Adam, he's in agony, all twisted up with desire for Becky yet not wanting to hurt old Mark either. Time to swiftly untangle this knot. Mark puts the cone down. 'I can't have her and she fancies you, now where's the problem?' He half-smiles, 'And don't deny that you fancy her. Not after the way you were looking at her this morning.' Adam grins sheepishly then leans back on the bed. 'Did you see her in that sweatshirt today?' He gives a low moan. 'There ought to be a law against her wearing that. I just went into the canteen for a second and there she was looking so . . . just blew everything out of my mind.'

'I know. I saw you gaping at her like a madman.'

'Was it that obvious?'

Mark almost enjoys this change of roles. For once he's setting Adam up.

'No,' he says kindly. 'I don't think anyone else really noticed.'

Adam shakes his head in wonderment. 'It's been so long since I saw a girl who meant anything. I mean, at those parties I'd see girls there but I was just pretending I'd fancied them.'

'I knew it,' says Mark.

'And I thought what's the matter with me? I even bought these dirty magazines just to test I was still – you know.'

'You never told me that.'

'No. Well, the tests were a bit inconclusive. I mean I did feel something but it was sort of far away. And then I saw Becky and everything just came roaring back. Suddenly I had all this energy. And my cold just evaporated away, of course. Mum thought it was due to her chicken soup . . .' Adam shakes his head. 'But does she want to go out with me?'

'Only one way to find out,' says Mark briskly, 'ring her. My mum won't mind. And it'll be easier here than at your house, won't it?'

'Much easier.'

'So go on then.' He adds by way of a spur,

'There are other boys after her you know. Like this guy in English, Clive, he loaned her this book of poetry today, and really thinks he's got his foot in the door now.'

'And has he?'

Mark shakes his head. 'Not yet. But you can't wait around. So go on, she's waiting for you.'

'How do you know?'

'I know.'

Adam sits up and Mark can see the idea growing in his head. Mark was right to push Adam. For if he doesn't get in there soon, someone else will. And Mark would much rather it was Adam than some other punk.

But then Adam falls back again. 'It's no good, mate. I haven't been out with a girl for so long that I don't know if – well, I don't know where to take her or anything. I'm really out of it all now.'

'You're taking her out for a meal at eight o'clock this Thursday,' says Mark. 'I'll arrange everything. All you've got to do is ring her. I'll do everything else. So GO ON!'

Adam jumps up, his head only an inch or two away from the ceiling now. And he suddenly seems to fill the whole room with his broad shoulders and big arms. He's taking everything from you, cries a nasty voice inside Mark which he immediately smothers. 'And you really don't mind?' says Adam, gazing down at him with such concern Mark has to look away. 'Just bloody ring her, will you?'

'With you coaching me, how can I fail?' cries Adam, and then he's off, thumping down the stairs. Mark picks up his orange cone. Earlier tonight he and Adam had passed some scaffolding with these cones flashing away. And seconds later one of them was under his jacket. Years ago he had a wardrobe full of cones, and he and Adam used to go regularly on raids. Now, all at once he's back collecting them again. He puts the cone underneath his window, moving it so it is exactly dead centre. He'll keep his notepad there and his diary.

Then he quietly opens his door to hear Adam saying. 'Hope you don't mind me ringing you but I wondered if you'd like to come out for a meal tomorrow night – with me,' he adds with a nervous laugh. Then after a slight pause, 'Great, would eight o'clock . . .' Mark closes his door again. Adam's home and dry. He knew he would be. And Mark's brought them together. Mark's played the only role open to him – matchmaker – good guy Mark. He can't stop now though, lots to arrange yet. He picks up his pad and immediately starts writing.

'And Vivien is turning into such a lovely girl.' Adam's mum looks at Adam significantly. But he knows how to blank her out. He's at home with his parents pretending to watch television when all he can think about is tomorrow night.

'You met her at cousin Anna's wedding, remember.'

Adam dimly remembers a girl squinting across a table at him who looked as if she had green teeth and had about as much sex appeal as a half eaten carrot.

'She and her mother are coming round tomorrow night just for an hour or two and – she's so looking forward to meeting you.'

'What a shame I'll be out then,' says Adam, his eyes never leaving the television screen.

'Out where?' demands his mother.

'Out with Mark.'

'Oh you can see Mark any time. Tomorrow night you're meeting Vivien. I'm sure Mark will understand.'

'I would give in gracefully if I were you,' says Adam's father with one of his sly grins. He and his mum always plonk themselves into these great heavy armchairs sitting right back in them as if they're waiting to be beamed up in space. Right now Adam can't think of anything he'd like better.

'You know your mother when she gets one of her ideas in her head,' continues his father, laughing indulgently. He's always saying things like this. He even made up a joke about her. 'What's the difference between your mother and a rottweiler – a rottweiler let's go.' And his mother had pretended to be cross with him and did her, 'Oh, the things he says,' act but really she loves him saying that.

It was total crap of course. When that smile drops off his face – that's when you've got to beware.

'I've promised Mark,' says Adam firmly. 'So I can't let him down. And I've no interest in meeting Vivien,' he adds. Then he quite deliberately stares down at his wrists and at those little scars, from the night he so ineptly tried to finish himself off.

It's awful really – the closer you are to someone the more you know exactly which buttons to press. Like now his parents voices are splintering away, just as he knew they would. For those scars are a reminder to Adam's parents that they aren't perfect and that through what they call 'their negligence' something awful nearly happened.

If Adam wasn't so desperate and so exasperated with them he'd never have called up that memory. Especially as it wasn't their fault. For they could hardly stand guard over him all day. And if they'd left him on his own for just five minutes he'd have done it. It really wasn't any big deal. Hadn't his insides already been blown to bits leaving nothing inside him, nothing that could ever be put together anyhow. So by slitting his wrists what was he doing – just blasting away useless rubble that's all. He certainly wasn't killing himself. He was dead inside already without her.

'Vivien's such a lovely girl,' mutters his mother 'and unattached.' But her tone suggests she knows she is defeated.

'I think Adam has a little more time yet before

settling down,' says his father. 'At the moment I should imagine a new motorbike looks more attractive than any young lady.' Adam gives a shy grin. Up to two weeks and three days ago his dad would have been completely right.

His dad is canny, shrewd – wise. And there was a time when his dad was, if not God, certainly God's deputy. He particularly liked the stories Dad would tell him at night. They were always about Yuncle and always had a moral, though never an obvious one. Adam's favourite was the one about Yuncle banging his head against a wall. On and on he went until someone asked, 'Yuncle, why do you bang your head against the wall like that?' And Yuncle looked up and said, 'because it feels so much better when I stop'.

Adam still loves that story even though he and his dad don't talk any more. Not really talk – well, it's too dangerous for a start. For there is so much of his life now that his parents know nothing about. So much he must keep away from their eyes.

Adam the double agent. That's what it often feels like. But tomorrow night overshadows everything else he's done. For then he'll be going out with a girl who isn't a Jew. How would his parents react to that. Adam can see his father's face tighten at the very idea.

Not that he would stop him. He'd just get his mum to fill the house with nice Jewish girls and wait impatiently for him to get Becky 'out of his system'. And – oh yes – his father would probably slip into the conversation something like, 'If you don't remember you're a Jew, someone else will.'

In a way his dad was right. And always when you were least expecting it – like one lunch-time at school, Adam was sitting on the sandwich table, which was the one nearest the door, with Mark and a couple of other guys when his teacher joined them. There followed this stilted conversation which kept breaking down into exhausted silences. And Adam, really because he couldn't think what else to say, said, 'I really like your tie sir.' And the teacher looked up and said, 'Well you should like it Adam. It's from one of your people, Marks and Spencer.'

But Marks and Spencer wasn't anything to do with Adam Rosen. So why single him out from the rest? Didn't he eat the same sandwiches (he'd insisted his mum stop bringing him fishballs after everyone asked what it was) laugh at the same jokes and listen to the same music as everyone else?

Yet, somehow, he was still different. He'd never forget that time in the art room when everyone was designing freaky Christmas cards. One guy had drawn a picture of this down-and-out Father Christmas looking dead miserable and underneath he'd written, 'It's no fun being a Yiddish Santa'.

When Adam saw that it was as if something very deep and strong inside him snapped open and he was crying, 'I find that really offensive,' before he realised it. And then he just stood there, seething with a strange kind of anger, that was so full of hurt and frustration he knew if he didn't turn away he'd start crying. So he walked out of the art room leaving this deathly silence behind him. Then the guy who'd drawn the picture came out with his drawing all screwed up in his hand, his face scorched with embarrassment. He started mumbling apologies until Adam said, 'No mate, I should be apologising to you. I was well out of order. I don't know what happened.' He still doesn't.

This was a real mystery. For he'd stopped believing – stopped even thinking of himself as a Jew years ago. Yet, somehow he couldn't dislodge this feeling of belonging, it was still a part of him.

But there are so many other parts to him now. Like the part which has seen Easy Rider seven times and listens to Iron Maiden and Guns and Roses over and over. And what about all the hundreds of hours he's spent with Mark and the rest of the gang. His parents don't know anything about these parts of him.

They never will.

Just like they'll never know about tomorrow night.

'In a way I'm dreading tonight' says Becky. She and Mark are sitting in the least trendy café in Cartford. Even at lunch-time half the tables are empty, the rest being occupied by solitary women

158

hunched over pots of tea, their shopping sprawled out over the other seats.

But as Becky says, 'At least you get served quietly,' and it is certainly private. 'I wish Adam and me were just going out for a drink,' continues Becky.

'Why?'

She starts to pour her tea. Every one of her fingers has a ring on it. One of the rings is light turquoise and looks quite valuable. Not that Mark would know much about that. But it's obvious to him that the other rings are about as expensive as the kind that come out of Christmas crackers. He decides, as soon as he can, he'll buy her a ring. A decent one. A friendship ring, he'll call it.

She puts the pot down. 'I won't pour yours yet,' she says, 'as you like it really strong.' Then she leans back. 'I keep thinking, what if we've got nothing to talk about.'

Mark smiles, 'I'm sure you'll think of something.'

'But that's it. I'm quite shy really. You wouldn't think that, would you?'

'No, not at all,' says Mark. He's laughing now.

'No, but honestly I am. And I'm just so worried I'll say something silly tonight. And then I'm really clumsy. I spilt this whole bottle of red wine at a party in the summer.'

'The last time I went out for a meal,' says Mark, 'it was round this girl's house and we're all sitting round the table when her mum brings in the biggest plate of spaghetti you've ever seen.'

'Oh no,' gasps Becky. 'What did you do?'

'Well her mum goes, "Just eat it as you do at home." And they all just dived in. But I was trying to chop it all up and be polite and hardly ate any of it. And then afterwards when I go over to the girl hoping for a little kiss, she says, "Did you know you've got sauce all over your face".'

Becky is laughing now. 'Oh Mark,' she says, 'I wish you were coming tonight. Why don't you?'

'No way,' says Mark. 'This is your night – you and Adam. And Adam's a really good guy and he won't care if you slurp your soup or burp or . . .'

'But that's the problem, isn't it. I don't really know anything about his personality. I just love his looks.' She leans forward. 'Don't tell Adam, but you know when I went into the wrong block?' Mark nods. 'Well, I saw him then, waiting to go into the hall. And straight away I said to myself, "Oh yes, that's the first target." But when I discovered I was in the wrong area I thought, oh, well that's it I'll never see him again. And then two hours later you come and introduce him to me. That's why I couldn't stop smiling at him. It just seemed too incredible.'

'You never told me that before,' says Mark.

'No, well it's silly really.'

Mark doesn't say anything for a moment. He's having another twinge of jealousy, quite a lengthy

160

twinge actually. They've been attacking him all day. Only to be expected. He starts pouring his tea. 'Should have put another teabag in here,' he mutters. 'If Adam weren't such a good friend of yours I don't know if I would go out with him like this,' says Becky. 'I mean I've only known you a few weeks but already I feel like we're real friends. I mean most friendships are just on the surface really, aren't they? But ours is different. It's special. And I couldn't have got through these last weeks without you, you know.' She reaches out and squeezes his hand. And Mark notices the waitress watching them. She probably thinks they're going out together. In a way they are. He's the daytime boyfriend, Adam the night shift.

'Oh, are you in tomorrow morning?' asks Becky.

'Yes.'

'I'll be on that phone then,' says Becky 'telling you all about tonight – and what a fool I made of myself.'

8 *You haven't been sending me roses, have you?*

Mark and Becky walk into English and assume their usual places in front of Lauren and Cathy. Mark turns round to say hello and Cathy and Lauren immediately beam their warmest smiles in his direction. Lauren then tops this by blowing him a kiss.

Then Lauren whispers, 'Look at him, just breaking his heart over her. Funny, you liked her but I never did.'

'It's not really her fault though is it,' says Cathy.

'Isn't it? Of all the people she could go out with she picks Adam, Mark's best mate.' She shakes her head, 'I hate to see poor Mark messed about like that. I really hate it.'

The door opens and Grant appears. Immediately there's a buzz of excitement. He's in his big mohair jumper and black jeans and looks like a cross between a rock star and a wayward librarian. He ambles to his desk, a faraway look on his face. What's he going to do today?

Last lesson they were in the video room when this woman burst in claiming she should really be there. She got really worked up while Grant just stared at her, chewing a piece of gum. Then after she flounced off Grant grinned conspiratorially at the class and said, 'Sexually frustrated I reckon, don't you?' Cathy couldn't imagine any of her old teachers saying that.

She liked his irreverence. And, despite herself, she enjoyed his lessons. He was unbearably arrogant, though, and he had this air of great superiority which she still hated. The first time she'd answered a question correctly he'd gaped at her in amazement as if to say, 'So you do know something, well what a surprise'. This look so angered her she answered every other question that lesson. Afterwards Lauren reckoned he'd been using some clever psychology on her. Cathy had her doubts.

Before their first lesson with Grant, Lauren had been on the phone for hours asking her what she should say when Grant asked her out. She'd finally decided she wouldn't go out with him but she'd be gracious and let him down gently.

So it was a real shock when Grant didn't say anything to her. Lauren hung around at the end of the lesson, convinced he was going to suddenly declare his undying love for her. But nothing happened.

163

And now if he favoured anyone in class it was Tricia Williams. And whenever Grant shared a joke with Tricia, Lauren sat stony-faced throughout.

Cathy knew Lauren wasn't breaking her heart over Grant – she just hated to lose an admirer, especially one as unusual as Grant.

Today, Grant solemnly places an apple on his desk. Cathy hopes he's not going to ask them to describe it. But instead he just says, 'I knew none of you would buy me an apple so I've bought one for myself, all right.'

He looks around. For the last few lessons he got them to arrange the desks into a horseshoe as he finds rows 'too threatening'. Today, though, he just stares ahead chewing a sweet – he's always chewing something – as if he's surveying them all. Then he says, 'All right ladies and gentlemen,' he stretches, 'today we're going to begin our look at the nineteenth century by examining the British mentality. Can you think of anything more exciting?' He gives one of his leery smiles. 'So I suggest we begin our study – by playing a game of croquet.'

Everyone is staring at him, confused. What did he just say? 'Well come on;' he says suddenly all alive and dynamic, 'we can't play croquet here can we. So follow me will you?'

Lauren is sitting in the library making notes. Grant sneaked this essay on them after an hilarious game

164

of croquet (which is much harder than it looks). And Lauren knows if she takes these books home they'll only stare reproachfully at her, for neglecting them so completely.

She had already made four pages of notes when Grant appeared. As always, he gives the impression of someone preoccupied with important matters. And Lauren expects him just to saunter past her. But instead he picks up one of the books she is copying from, raises an eyebrow, then gives her a rather puzzled smile as if to say, 'What are you reading this for' – and disappears.

Moments later he returns spinning a small green book down the table at her. 'You might find this useful.'

Lauren looks up. 'Oh, thank you.' She examines the book rather self-consciously as he stands watching her. And he has the most extraordinary way of looking at you. It's as if he can peer right into your head, and read your every thought.

'On your own?' he asks suddenly.

'Yes, Cathy's gone to Radleys'

'Good.' He then sits down opposite her. The library is practically empty and most of the students are in the corner, clustered round the teletext. He doesn't say anything at first, just taps his fingers on the table. It's a little habit of his. He often does it in class, sometimes when he's talking. It's as if his fingers are beating out a rhythm all of their

165

own which has nothing to do with the rest of his body.

'What are you doing tonight?' he asks lightly, while still tapping his fingers.

'Nothing in particular.'

'Well, you are now. I'll pick you up at eight o'clock at the top of your road.'

Lauren's face is one big smile. So he does still fancy her. He was just waiting for the right moment. Well, who can blame him. Still, Lauren doesn't know if she wants to go out with him or not. He's intriguing and it would be a bit of prestige – on the other hand would she want a whole evening of him?

'I don't normally go out on Thursday nights,' she says with a coy smile. Make him suffer a bit too. 'But if I did go out with you, where exactly would we go?'

There's a glint of amusement in his eyes as he says, 'To Lombards, where else?'

'Oh, like last time, you mean,' she says with a mischievous smile. If he wants to take her out he's going to have to work a bit. But she decides she will go out with him just the once, just for the experience, and so she can say she's been to Lombards. To her surprise he stops smiling and says, 'I have really tried to apologise to you for that.'

And he says this in such a serious tone she finds herself asking, 'You haven't been sending me flowers and cards have you?' The question is out

166

before she's realised it. He gets up and looks embarrassed.

'Desperate men resort to desperate clichés,' he says. Then he seems to recover himself and says, 'So I'll pick you up at eight o'clock at the top of your road?'

'Yes, all right.' Her voice is dull and flat but he doesn't seem to notice. He only turns back to say, 'Not a word to anyone, not even Cathy.'

A minute ago she'd have found those words exciting. Now all she can think is she'd so wanted the card sender to be Jason. But it isn't. He doesn't really care. He doesn't feel what she feels.

From around the teletext come gales of loud derisive laughter. Lauren stares at them furiously. All blokes. Typical of them to be so happy when . . . She'd really made herself believe it was Jason. Waves of dark, helpless anger sweep over her. WHY ISN'T IT JASON? WHY?

URGENT MEMO TO ALL ANIMAL RIGHTS MEMBERS FROM CATHY

ON FRIDAY, 11 OCTOBER A 6-HOUR DEMONSTRATION WILL TAKE PLACE OUTSIDE RADLEYS 11.00–17.00 HRS

THE CHAIRMAN OF RADLEYS IS DUE AT 11.30 SO YOU WILL BE NEEDED ANY TIME PAST 11.30

THIS IS OUR BIG CHANCE TO MAKE

THOUSANDS OF PEOPLE TURN AGAINST EATING MEAT. BUT FOR THIS TO BE ANY GOOD WE MUST HAVE DEMONSTRATORS THROUGHOUT THE ENTIRE SIX HOURS. THEREFORE, PLEASE TAKE THE TIME OFF LEC-TURES, DO ANYTHING *BUT YOU MUST BE THERE TO MAKE THIS A SUCCESS*.

Cathy is just underlining the last sentence when the phone rings. 'I'll get it,' she calls. Not that anyone else can even hear the phone. Her mum and Katie are sitting in the lounge with HIM watching a video he's chosen. Unsurprisingly it's one of those brain-dead films which mainly consist of cars that keep catching fire and just flip over when people run away from them.

Cathy picks up the phone. It's Lauren.

'Hi, how are you darlin'?' Cathy asks settling back in her chair for one of their long chats.

'Oh, I'm fine,' says Lauren in a tone of voice that suggests she is definitely not fine.

'What's wrong? Come on, tell me.'

'Nothing – except, I found out who's been send-ing me those flowers – Grant.'

'Grant – are you sure?'

'He told me in the library this afternoon. So you were wrong, it wasn't Jason.'

'I really thought it was.'

'Yeah, well now you know.'

'Lauren – I'm sorry.'

'Don't be. Grant has asked me out tonight.'

Another shock! Cathy's ears are ringing. 'Asked you out when?'

'This afternoon in the Library. We're going to Lombards.'

'But is that wise?'

'Honestly, Cathy why do you have to make such a big deal out of everything. I'm going out for one evening with Grant, to *the* nightclub, that's all. He's an interesting man and I shall enjoy going out with him once.' Lauren emphasises the once.

'Say he wants to go out with you again?'

'I'll tell him no.'

'But won't that be difficult, him being your teacher.' Cathy is pacing backwards and forwards with the phone now.

'No, it won't. Oh, I wish I hadn't told you now. Look I've just got to go out tonight all right?'

'Why don't we go out then?'

'Because I'm going out with Grant. Anyway I like older men. At least they're not users.'

'Lauren, listen, Jason may not have sent you those cards but he does care about you. I'm convinced about that.'

The lounge door opens. Giles is standing in the doorway. 'I'm talking,' snaps Cathy before turning her back on him.

'Well, can you try not to pull the cord quite so

169

hard,' he says. 'Those phones can all too easily be pulled out of the socket.'

Cathy whirls round, 'It's not your phone,' she cries, quite forgetting all her promises to mum last week, that she'd at least be polite to him. He glares at her before slamming the door and running off to tell tales to mum. Oh damn. Still, she has more important things to worry about now.

'Lauren, sorry about that. Look I'm going to ring Jason.'

'Don't you dare.'

'Yes, I am. This has gone on long enough. I'll just tell him . . .'

'Cathy if you speak to him about me I'll never forgive you. I mean that. Did you hear me?'

Cathy's mum opens the door. 'When you've finished on the phone can I have a word with you please?'

'Yes, Mum,' says Cathy. The door closes noiselessly and Lauren is ranting on . . . 'Don't want him to think I'm crawling to him. Promise me you won't ring Jason. Promise me.'

'All right,' says Cathy wearily. 'I won't ring Jason, I promise. But tonight just be . . .'

'I'll be all right, darlin'.' Lauren's voice is gentler. 'Now I'd better go. But remember what you promised.'

'I'll remember.' The phone clicks off. Cathy stands thinking for a moment, then she starts ringing Jez's number.

'You're a man of courage Jason, aren't you?' asks Jez.

Jason's laughter crackles down the phone. 'What are you on about now matey?'

'I'm inviting Jason the Bold to join me in sampling,' he lowers his voice to a whisper, 'some of my dad's home-made wine.'

'If it's anything like his last wine . . .'

'It is, only stronger. Much stronger. So you probably can't handle it.'

'Last time, as I remember, it was you who ended up paralytic and generally out of your skull?'

Jez laughs but he isn't smiling. He's finding this whole phone call distinctly painful.

'Okay, mate, you're on,' says Jason. 'I'll be round in about an hour and I'll bring a couple of videos. Any requests?'

'No, I'll trust your taste.'

'I'll see what I can do,' laughs Jason.

'Anyone else coming round?'

'No, this is strictly exclusive,' says Jez quickly.

'All right then, see you in a bit mate,' says Jason.

An unusually grim-faced Jez stares out of the window. The sky is full of heavy black clouds. Any second now there's going to be one almighty downpour.

He hates hassle and always walks away from arguments. It's only Cathy ringing up tonight that's finally stirred him into telling Jason – what? That what he'd told Jason about Lauren and him was a pile of crap. But that it wasn't meant nastily. It was just an ego trip for Jez really. But his lies had – no, they hadn't caused Jason and Lauren to break up had they? They'd have split up anyway. He just speeded the process up a little that's all. Jason may think differently of course. And Jez wouldn't blame him, if he did.

The clouds are growing even darker, so dark you know they've just got to burst open any second now.

Jez looks away and there for the first time that evening he laughs. He's dreading tonight and yet he's laughing because if you don't laugh well, you just disappear, don't you?

'I've booked the table for eight o'clock,' says Mark. 'I asked for somewhere reasonably off-centre.'

'Right, right,' says Adam. Then he takes another swig of lager. 'Just to take the tension away,' he explains, 'and to get myself swinging.' They both laugh nervously. Then Adam gets up and starts pacing around Mark's bedroom, putting his right hand in is pocket as he does so. He wants to saunter into the restaurant like that. So it's best he practises.

He'd only bought these trousers yesterday with a white shirt and tie – all Mark's idea. Go for a smart image he'd said. He's probably right. Just provided Becky doesn't expect this kind of look every time. Then he smiles, who says there's going to be a next time?

He'd been worried that his parents might become suspicious when he left looking – for him – amazingly smart. So he told them, 'Everyone's dressing up tonight,' and his parents just nodded approvingly and then exchanged glances which meant, he's coming out of his scruffy phase at last.

Adam looks at his watch again. 'Exactly 7.30 pm, Mark. Now what time's the taxi picking her up?'

Mark picks up his pad and reads, 'Taxi arriving 7.45 pm. I asked for a driver who is a non-smoker as Becky doesn't like cars that smell of fags. Scheduled to arrive 7.55 pm.'

'I'd better go in a couple of minutes then,' says Adam. 'How long do you reckon it'll take me walking, twenty minutes?'

Mark nods, 'At the outside.' Then he stands back and stares at Adam appraisingly. Adam looks the business and Mark feels a surge of pride about that. For Adam relied completely on him.

'I'd forgotten to give you these,' he says. He picks up from the dressing-table two cuff links with eyes on them. 'I'd been saving these up for a special occasion,' he says. 'And while you're putting them on I'll give your shoes an extra polish.'

Two gulps of lager later Adam is finally ready to leave. He totters slightly to the door.

'Will you be all right?'

173

'Yeah, fine. Thanks for everything mate. I owe you one.'

'I'll send my bill round in the morning.'

Adam smiles, then says, 'I'm not sweating am I?'

'No.'

'I'm sweating something evil inside.'

They solemnly shake hands. 'I'll give you a ring tomorrow morning,' says Adam. 'With all the gory details.'

Then he's off, down the stairs, his right hand firmly in his trouser pocket.

'Go for it, mate.' Mark calls after him. Adam turns back and waves. Mark can hear his mum calling him. But he doesn't want to talk to anyone now. Instead he slowly walks back into his bedroom, closing the door tightly behind him.

Lauren arrives home to find a fourth 'Sorry' card and red rose waiting for her. She tears up this card and the three other cards she'd so reverently kept in her dressing table. And she goes on tearing up the cards into smaller and smaller bits.

She wants to chuck the rose into the bin, too, but fears this might make her mum even more curious. 'And you still don't know who it is,' her mum had asked earlier this evening, all bright-eyed and excited.

'No,' replies Lauren, wearily. These cards aren't exciting any more. In fact they seem rather nauseating now, like those three-foot cards with a panda on the front looking all bashful and saying, 'I love you'. They're just too much. More like a joke really. Perhaps that's what they are. Grant's got a strange sense of humour.

She gets ready to go out in a kind of trance. Then her dad calls her. He stands at the bottom of the stairs, chomping his apple pie – he rarely manages to stay seated for an entire meal – watching her descend saying, 'Well if I were twenty years younger I'd go for you. Don't you look beautiful.'

'If you were twenty years younger I might go for you,' says Lauren. 'No make that ten years.' Her dad is beaming all over his not inconsiderable face now. And seconds later he's reaching into his wallet. He hands her a twenty pound note, 'Just to buy your friends a drink from me. It is the usual crowd tonight isn't it? Cathy and . . .'

'Oh yes, that's right,' says Lauren stuffing the twenty pound note into her wallet. If she'd told him she was going out for a date he'd only have given her five pounds.

'Your mother's had some good news,' he says.

Her mum's face is pink with pleasure. 'Lost ten pounds,' she says.

'Just another ten to go,' says her dad.

Recently her mum had said she wanted a new car. Dad had said he'd buy her the car of her choice when she lost twenty pounds and went back to the weight she'd been when he'd married her.

175

'That's really good, Mum,' says Lauren opening the door. It's raining quite hard and her mum says, 'You'll have to take her to Cathy's in the car, John.'

'No, no, it's all right,' says Lauren hastily, 'I feel like a walk. I've got a bit of a headache.'

'I thought you looked a bit flushed,' says her mum. 'Should you be going out then?'

'Oh, yes, a bit of air will do me good,' says Lauren quickly putting up her umbrella. 'Bye then.'

'I know you won't be late,' her father calls after her.

She's a few minutes early but he's waiting there for her. She thought she might enjoy the secrecy of all this but she doesn't. Instead she feels as if she's watching herself on a television programme. Nothing that happens tonight seems to belong to her.

Grant leans across and opens the door. 'Let me put your umbrella in the back,' he says. 'You look soaked.' He's wearing the same jacket he wore the night she met him. Only this time he's also wearing a hideously bright tie. He sees her looking at the tie, then smiles. 'What do you think?'

'It's a bit loud.'

'Lombards insist on their patrons wearing ties so I insist on wearing the ugliest tie I can find. It's taken me several days to find this.'

And Lauren could imagine him asking bewildered assistants to show him their ugliest tie, with that strange pinched smile on his face as he did so.

'Once every gentleman had to wear a wig, now it's a tie,' he declares.

'I can imagine you in a wig,' says Lauren suddenly.

'Can you?' he says, and then for a second he moves closer to her and Lauren thinks he is going to kiss her. She feels herself tense up. But instead he just whispers, 'Glad you could make it.'

Then there's silence, broken only by the windscreen wipers whirling energetically backwards and forwards and the rain streaming outside.

'By the way, thank you for the cards and flowers,' says Lauren. 'But really there's no need to send any more. In fact I'd rather you didn't.'

'I haven't been sending you any cards,' says Grant and he sounds quite indignant. 'In fact I don't believe I've sent anyone a card in my life. A disgusting habit.'

'But earlier you said you did.'

'No, I didn't,' he paused. 'I just implied it.' And he gives one of his sudden bursts of laughter. And then Lauren laughs too, but even louder.

She knows who sent those cards, those wonderful cards. How could she have torn them up. And how could she have thought they were from anyone else. Cathy was right. It had to be Jason, didn't it? JASON. That's what the windscreen wipers are

177

singing over and over – JASON! JASON! JASON! JASON.'

'I'm sorry if I misled you,' says Grant. 'However, although I may not give cards I do have other uses.' He picks out an envelope from the glove department and throws it into her lap.

'Open it,' he comments.

Inside Lauren finds tickets – two tickets for next Saturday. 'It's a new film so you can't have seen it,' he says.

'It's by the director of *Blue Velvet*. Have you seen *Blue Velvet*?'

'No.'

'I can see I've got some work to do on you,' he says. He makes it sound as if she's still his pupil and this is part of her course. But then he puts his arm around her, 'I shall enjoy my work though,' he says.

He's pushing too hard. He can't just assume she'll go out with him again. She should tell him. This is just a one-off. And she loves someone else. JASON JASON. The windscreen wipers are roaring his name now.

But she doesn't say anything. And his arm remains around her shoulder like a clamp. Usually she'd say, 'Move your arm.' But you can't talk like that to your teacher. She peers outside. The rain is beating furiously against the window. Normally she likes looking out on the rain. It makes her feel all safe and cosy. But now it just makes her feel totally lost.

The windscreen wipers are only whispering his name now. It's growing fainter and fainter.

And now she can't hear it at all.

All she can hear is her heart thumping.

Friends Forever 2 – *Break Out* is available now in *Teens*.

Also by Pete Johnson

FRIENDS FOREVER 2 : BREAK OUT

The exciting sequel to *Friends Forever 1 : No Limits*, BREAK OUT is also available from *Teens · Mandarin*.

Why does Adam have to sneak out of his bedroom at night?
Who is sending Lauren those roses?
Why does Jez get into a fight?
What happens when Cathy organises a demonstration?
Why does Jason nearly lose his job?

"Pete Johnson's work is changing while his teenage voice is always authentic."

Glasgow Herald

Pete Johnson

ONE STEP BEYOND

Sometimes you're walking right on the edge and don't even realise it.

Like Alex. He's waited five years to take revenge on Mr Stones.

And Natasha. She's always done what her parents tell her – until the day she turns sixteen.

Then there's Yorga. He has a brilliant idea to stop the hated Casuals taking over his town.

Just three of the people who don't realise they're right on the edge – until they take one step beyond.

A collection of eight dazzling stories of love, revenge, laughter and horror.

"Pete Johnson, an author who can pinpoint what is distinctive about his readers . . . without being either patronising or strait-jacketed by their demands."

Sunday Times

A selected list of titles available from Teens

While every effort is made to keep prices low, it is sometimes necessary to increase prices at short notice. Mandarin Paperbacks reserves the right to show new retail prices on covers which may differ from those previously advertised in the text or elsewhere.

The prices shown below were correct at the time of going to press.

☐	7497 0095 5	**Among Friends**	Caroline B Cooney £2.99
☐	7497 0145 5	**Through the Nightsea Wall**	Otto Coontz £2.99
☐	7497 0582 5	**The Promise**	Monica Hughes £2.99
☐	7497 0171 4	**One Step Beyond**	Pete Johnson £2.50
☐	7497 0281 8	**The Homeward Bounders**	Diana Wynne Jones £2.99
☐	7497 0312 1	**The Changeover**	Margaret Mahy £2.99
☐	7497 0473 X	**Shellshock**	Anthony Masters £2.99
☐	7497 0323 7	**Silver**	Norma Fox Mazer £3.50
☐	7497 0325 3	**The Girl of his Dreams**	Harry Mazer £2.99
☐	7497 0280 X	**Beyond the Labyrinth**	Gillian Rubinstein £2.50
☐	7497 0558 2	**Frankie's Story**	Catherine Sefton £2.50
☐	7497 0009 2	**Secret Diary of Adrian Mole**	Sue Townsend £2.99
☐	7497 0333 4	**Plague 99**	Jean Ure £2.99
☐	7497 0147 1	**A Walk on the Wild Side**	Robert Westall £2.99

All these books are available at your bookshop or newsagent, or can be ordered direct from the publisher. Just tick the titles you want and fill in the form below.

Mandarin Paperbacks, Cash Sales Department, PO Box 11, Falmouth, Cornwall TR10 9EN.

Please send cheque or postal order, no currency, for purchase price quoted and allow the following for postage and packing:

UK including BFPO   £1.00 for the first book, 50p for the second and 30p for each additional book ordered to a maximum charge of £3.00.

Overseas including Eire   £2 for the first book, £1.00 for the second and 50p for each additional book thereafter.

NAME (Block letters) ....

ADDRESS ....

....

☐ I enclose my remittance for ....

☐ I wish to pay by Access/Visa Card Number

Expiry Date